HOT CHICKEN

A SUNDAY BROTHERS NOVELLA

MAY ARCHER

Cover Design: Beth Cranford
Editing: One Love Editing

ISBN: 978-1-964685-23-6

All the good bits are theirs, and any mistakes are my own!

INTRODUCTION

Once upon a time, in the town of Little Pippin Hollow, Vermont, Hawk Sunday spotted a silly ceramic rooster on a crowded table at the Annual Craft and Rummage Sale… and a whole flock of *hot* Sunday summer shenanigans ensued!

Hot Chicken is a collection of five steamy, interconnected stories where we catch up with each of our Sunday couples (Knox and Gage, Webb and Luke, Porter and Theo, Hawk and Jack, *and* Uncle Drew and Marco!) as they navigate the gloriously messy realities of their own happily-ever-afters.

Get ready to swoon as big questions are finally asked, sigh as tiny (baby) secrets are revealed, and snort-laugh at the ridiculous lengths these men will go to for love. Because when it comes to the Sunday Brothers, there's no such thing as too much chaos, too much passion, too much romance…

Or too much Hot Chicken.

Note that Hot Chicken *is a 36k word collection best enjoyed by those who've already read the Sunday Brothers series. It originally appeared as a Patreon serial, and no new content has been added.*

~A NOTE FROM MAY~

GINORMOUS THANKS to everyone who made this book possible:

My **patrons**, who read and commented on each chapter all summer…

Lucy, who came up with the perfect title, and made the story so much better…

Beth for the adorbs cover, and **Jodi** for her eagle eyes…

And most of all, **you** for loving these Sundays and wanting more. THANK YOU!

Enjoy your visit to the Hollow!
Love,
~May

JACK AND HAWK

CHAPTER ONE

JACK

THE LITTLE PIPPIN HOOKERS ANNUAL CRAFT AND RUMMAGE SALE was many things to many people.

For the civic-minded, like my fiancé, Hawk, it was a chance to support the community since all proceeds benefited local LGBTQ outreach programs.

For me, it was a chance to finally spend a day with my man—even if it meant we were toiling over donated kitchenware side by side at the Dishes and Doo-Dads table. We'd both been incredibly busy this summer, and couple time was at a premium.

For bargain hunters like Hawk's uncle Drew, it was a chance to add to his wardrobe, even if it resulted in his boyfriend's grumpy objections ("I don't care how cheap it is, Drew! We're supposed to be downsizing so we can buy a smaller place, remember?") with a sunshiny rebuke ("But Marco, baby… *it's for charity!*").

For the town's gossip hounds—okay, fine, *all* of us—it was a prime opportunity to dish and be dished about.

And for certain otherwise rational folks, it was an opportunity to be perfectly *irrational* about kitchen décor.

Case in point… the cock.

"Oh my God!" Teagan Curran gasped. He stared into the half-disintegrated cardboard box of kitchen décor on the grass, which he'd been unpacking onto the Dishes and Doo-Dads table.

The sun shone down on the top of his head, turning his hair from its usual auburn to a bright, coppery shine. People at nearby tables chatted excitedly about the beautiful morning, even though the heat was already sweltering.

"This is epic!"

I glanced up from my own critically important task of affixing colored price labels to the table full of tchotchkes. "What is?"

"This!" Teagan lifted out a ceramic cookie jar and held it aloft, not unlike Simba on Pride Rock.

I wrinkled my nose. *This* appeared to be a rooster-shaped cookie jar. It was large and squat, with a white body, an orange beak, a chip on one wing, and somnolent eyes that suggested it had been napping. It also had a truly *enormous* set of red wattles.

Cute… if you liked that sort of thing. Epic, though? Not so much.

Hawk, who'd been cleaning a decade's worth of dust off some donated teacups, glanced up. We exchanged a quick smirk, and when Hawk looked away, I caught him fighting a grin that made my whole dusty, sweaty morning worthwhile.

Teagan's friend Fern set another donation box beside the table and peered at the rooster. "Looks like an '80s dust catcher to me," she said with an eye roll. "Oooh, unless there's money inside?"

"Hush, Fernella," Teagan chided, covering the rooster's ears. "He'll hear you."

"He?" Fern repeated. "Oh, Teagan, honestly…"

"What? He might be a mere decorative object to you, but to me, he has a very distinct psychic presence." Teagan lifted his chin stubbornly, which set his long, red ponytail swinging. "He's yearning for something."

"Aw." Hawk's kind brown eyes shone with sympathy. My man hated to hear of a creature in need, whether it was a fellow human, a pregnant cat... or apparently poultry-shaped crockery. "What do you think he's yearning for? Chicken feed, maybe? Oh, or cookies since he's a cookie jar?"

I snorted. "Maybe air-conditioning, to escape this heat wave?" I wiped the side of my face against the shoulder of my T-shirt, and Hawk, because he was Hawk, gave me a distinctly *interested* up-down look that made my heart beat faster.

"Maybe a best friend who's not a drama llama?" Fern suggested, shooting Teagan a grin. "I know that's what *I* yearn for."

Teagan's lips twitched. "Mmmkay, first of all, you *love* my drama, Fernalicious. You *live* for my drama. The universe created you as a vessel for my drama, as it does with all best friend pairings, just as it created me to be a vessel for yours—"

"Oh, ew. Fucking gross." Fern shuddered and retched. "You just made it so weird, Teagan. Why are you like this?"

Hawk covered his laughter with his hand.

"And second of all." Teagan's ponytail swished triumphantly. "This isn't drama at all. It's me accessing my latent talents." He narrowed his eyes. "Which, as my best friend, you should be *encouraging*."

"Your latent talents?" Hawk tilted his head, plainly confused. "What talents?"

"Well, since you asked..." Teagan began, giving Hawk a friendly smile.

"Oh, God, now you've done it," Fern moaned. She stepped between Teagan and Hawk. "There was a fortune-teller booth at the Averill Union end-of-school carnival a few weeks ago, Hawk. And of course, our Teagan here had to ask a billion questions about the lotions and potions and crystals the lady was selling—"

Teagan squawked. "Because I'm a friendly person who seeks *knowledge*, Fern!"

"And then *buy* a billion lotions and potions—"

"Because the scent of palo santo is relaxing!"

"And the woman told Teagan he was an empath who needed to work on 'unlocking his skills,'" Fern concluded with an eye roll. "If he'd bought a couple more crystals, she might have convinced him he was the reincarnation of George Washington."

"Excuse you." Teagan folded his arms over his chest and stepped around her. "Master Iris said I'm at least a Class Four empath and that I'm *particularly* attuned to feelings and vibrations many humans cannot sense." He gave an injured sniff. "My husband agreed. I bet *he'd* believe me if I told him I could sense this rooster's feelings."

"Let's be honest, babe," Fern said mildly. "John would have agreed about the George Washington thing, too, if you gave him your big heart eyes when you told him."

This was absolutely true, as anyone who'd been around the pair would know. Teagan's burst of startled laughter said he knew it, too.

I pressed my lips together to hide my smile.

"The man looks forward to your road trip karaoke," Fern said, holding up a finger as if counting off evidence, "though we both know your rendition of 'All Too Well' is a musical crime. He also once told me with absolute sincerity that you were sexier than Timothée Chalamet." She held up a second finger. "And he's taking you on a three-week Sourdough Experience in Northern Europe next month as a belated honeymoon." A third finger. "I adore John, and I'd trust him with just about anything, but he's not exactly a reliable reporter when it comes to your, ah… talents, boo."

Teagan laughed again. As if called by the sound, his

husband, John, glanced over from where he'd been chatting with Webb Sunday by the Sunday Orchard table, just out of earshot. His questioning eyes met Teagan's, and Teagan blew him a kiss. The burly man blushed beet red beneath his beard but returned Teagan's adoring look and stood just a little taller as he turned back to his conversation with Webb.

I chuckled to myself. Yeah, I could definitely see John agreeing that Teagan was an empath. And much like the stupid ceramic rooster itself, this sort of blind loyalty was kinda cute... but also not really my thing.

Don't get me wrong, I adored Hawk. Utterly, completely adored him. His happiness was my happiness, as evidenced by the five (yes, *five*) cats I was now co-parenting, the enormous library (complete with lube cubbies) I'd built for my novel-loving fiancé, and the fact that more and more of Hawk's clothes ended up in my closet since his own had become a yarn cache, and I never dreamed of complaining.

Still, there were limits. Believing that one's beloved could sense the thoughts and feelings of a ceramic rooster was a bridge too far. A line between a partnership founded on true love and... well, unrestrained, over-the-top devotion.

"Wait, back up, Teagan," Hawk said eagerly. "Tell me more about what the rooster's thinking!"

I snorted.

"Well." Teagan set the bird in the center of the table. "I can't really read its thoughts. I can only sense its energy. And it wants something. Misses something. Needs... something."

"Huhhhhh." Hawk tilted his head and stared at the rooster, transfixed.

Meanwhile, Fern gave Teagan's arm a gentle pat. "You have many actual gifts, babydoll. You're an amazing friend. A bread-making champion. An encyclopedia of random television shows. A damn good teacher. Pretty much the only thing I *don't* think you can do is read the psychic vibrations of kitchen crockery." She flipped her hand casually in the direction of the rooster, then stopped and gave the rooster a suspicious glare. "Although I have to admit, if there were ever an inanimate object that *did* have a presence, it might be this one."

"You know, my uncle Drew had an antique chicken just like this one when I was a kid. He once told me ceramic poultry decorations were the Live-Laugh-Love sign of the '80s and '90s. He's like a little piece of history," Hawk said with perfect sincerity. "I bet this little guy's been sitting in someone else's kitchen for decades."

I snorted. I found it highly amusing when Hawk referred to the 1990s—a decade I remembered quite well—as "antique" and "history." His older brothers weren't quite as amused.

"He probably has," Teagan agreed. "And when you think about it, doesn't it make sense that an object would soak up the energy of the place where it's been staying? And be sort of *yearning* to find that same energy?" He gave Fern a challenging look. "I seem to recall you having a pair of stinky softball socks back in college that you wouldn't put in the laundry so that the 'luck wouldn't wash off.'"

"That's different." Fern hesitated. Frowned. "Though I'm not quite sure how."

"Uh-huh," Teagan said smugly. "It's okay. I accept your apology for questioning my abilities."

She huffed out a laugh. "Right. So, *Master Teagan*, you're saying that this... cockadoodle cookie jar has soaked up '90s kitchen energy, and now it's hungry?"

Teagan stared at the rooster for a minute in concentration. "Not hungry for food," he murmured. "More like..." Teagan's eyes widened, and he cleared his throat. He shot a glance at his handsome husband, bit his lip, and full-on blushed. "Er. You know. On second thought, maybe I'm projecting. He's probably just hungry for cookies. Like you said."

Fern laughed, and so did I. But Hawk was giving the bird a sweet, thoughtful, sympathetic look again. "The poor thing really needs a good home, doesn't he?"

I smiled softly. The man had the biggest heart in New England and endless love to give. I was so fucking lucky he was mine to love and care for in return.

Because he was, I ducked under the table and grabbed an insulated water bottle. Then I pressed the bottle into Hawk's hands, wrapped my arms around his waist from behind, and pulled him against me. "Drink, baby," I instructed softly. "It's fucking hot out here."

Hawk smiled a little as he obeyed, and despite the July heat and humidity making both of us sticky, he leaned into my chest like he relished the closeness as much as I did.

It had been an incredibly busy few weeks for both of us. Tourist season was in full swing, and despite hiring extra servers and cooks, I was at Panini Jack's late every night.

Meanwhile, Hawk was up early each day working on new environmental initiatives for the town, taking a summer class at Hannabury, planning the Craft and Rummage Sale with the Little Pippin Hookers, our local fiber arts and community service group, *and* working shifts alongside me at the restaurant.

On the rare occasions when we were both home, we took care of our cats (who, Hawk insisted, required adequate stimulation for proper brain development), did household chores, and tackled some of the myriad decisions required to plan our upcoming fall wedding.

It shouldn't have been possible to miss someone you shared a bed with each night, someone you lived your life beside, but there was a difference between side by side and *together*.

It had been a hot minute since Hawk and I had gone hiking, since we'd made time for him to give me a hand-waving, eye-rolling, hand-clasping retelling of his latest *Pride and Prejudice* fanfic, or even since I'd held his gorgeous body against mine like this for longer than a few minutes.

Which meant *my* body was now having a predictable reaction to having the sexiest man in the universe back in my arms where he belonged.

I set my chin on his shoulder, wanting to keep him as close as possible for as long as possible, and followed his gaze down to the rooster.

It *was* a cute little beast, I decided. Harmless-looking and sweet. The sort of thing your grandmother would like. But then I made the mistake of looking at its eyes.

At first glance, I'd thought the rooster looked sleepy with its half-shut eyes. Now, though, the thing looked decidedly awake and really fucking smirky. It probably didn't help that someone had daubed gold craft paint on the bird's eyes, which made them glow in the light. The red wattles hanging below its beak were cartoonishly large and lopsided and frozen mid-flop in a way that made them look like... like... well, like a pair of scarlet balls hanging off its face. And once I'd thought the words, I couldn't unsee it.

"That thing is mildly terrifying," I joked. "And possibly pornographic."

"Jack." Hawk—my darling, my best friend, my future husband—turned his head and gave me an admonishing glance. "Don't be mean." He grabbed the rooster from the table and clutched it to his chest protectively. "He's *delightful.*"

"He?" I repeated with a feeling of growing dread. "Bird, no. Tell me you don't actually believe—"

"Alright." Fern finished unpacking her box and dusted her hands. "Let's get some of this stuff priced up before the crowd arrives! How much for the cock? Think we could get five dollars if Tee does his *Master Teagan* thing and tells a tale about its energy?"

Hawk gave her an admonishing look. "Fern. A little

respect, please. Sir Pecksworth is a priceless symbol of good fortune who deserves a good home."

Fern blinked at him. So did I.

"Baby, you're talking about the rooster like he's real," I pointed out, squeezing his waist tighter.

Hawk whirled in my arms. "Because he is!" he said passionately. Then he blinked like his outburst had startled even himself. "I, uh, I mean, he's a *real*… ceramic rooster." He set the thing down on the table, then frowned and picked it up again. "Whose name happens to be Sir Pecksworth."

"Oh my gosh." Teagan stared at Hawk with wide eyes. "Hawk's an empath, too."

Hawk scowled. "No! Don't be silly. I just…" He bit his lip. "I feel like Pecky's… lucky and that he really wants to come home with me and Jack." He turned liquid eyes up to mine. "Okay?"

I opened my mouth. Then I closed it again.

I might have bought our house originally, but since it hadn't been a home until Hawk had lived there, too, it was, without a doubt, *our* house. As such, Hawk *never* asked my permission when bringing things home, nor would I ever want him to. See also: the aforementioned yarn closet.

The only time Hawk had ever asked if we could *keep* something, it had involved our cats, which made sense since they were, you know, *alive*. So I wasn't sure whether to laugh or be weirded out that he was asking permission now.

"Yes. Of course," I said. "Whatever you want, baby."

Hawk beamed up at me, love shining in his eyes.

Apparently, empaths and magical, cursed roosters weren't the hard limit I'd thought they were.

Hawk pushed up on his tiptoes, wrapped his free arm around my neck, and gave me a soft kiss that reminded me he was mine forever, no matter how busy we both got.

"I love you, Jack Wyatt," he whispered against my lips,

which made me *feel* magical, too. "I really, *really* love you. Every day. All the time."

I wrapped my arms around his waist. Was it a little odd that the ceramic chicken was pressed between us? Maybe. Would I let it stop me from kissing the man I loved? Fuck no. "Same, baby. Same. So let's take Pecky home and feed him."

CHAPTER TWO

HAWK

WHEN JACK and I walked through the front door of our house several hours later, arms loaded with bags, five furry faces immediately trotted over to greet us.

"Lydia Sunday," Jack chided when the tiny tortoiseshell clawed at one of the grocery bags he carried while Jane, Lizzy, Mary, and Potato twined around his ankles. "Honestly, ladies. You'd think you'd never been fed in your fucking lives."

"I'll feed them," I offered, unwrapping Sir Pecksworth and setting him on the counter by the stove with a fond pat. "If you put the groceries away."

Jack glanced up from where he was fiddling with the window air conditioner unit and gave the cookie jar a smirk and a headshake.

"Deal," he said. "I'll even make up a batch of that marinade you like so we can grill some..." He gave Pecky a significant look, then shot me a wink as I scooped dry cat food into bowls. "C-H-I-C-K-E-N for dinner."

Then the air conditioner let out a blast of cold air, and he sighed happily.

I felt a slow smile spread over my face as I watched him.

In the golden-hour sunshine streaming through the

window, with the cool breeze blowing his hair and making his sweaty T-shirt stick to his chest, Jack Wyatt was impossibly handsome. The sight of those strong shoulders, the stubbled jaw, would never get old. Would never cease to make my heart skip and my mouth water.

Wanting this man, wanting simply to be near him, had consumed my every thought for years. And now, here I was, not only sharing Jack's bed but his home and his life. Planning a future with him. Allowed and encouraged to reach out and touch him, *kiss* him, any damn time I wanted. I got to sleep with his arms around me. He'd agreed to be my personal Mr. Darcy, forever and ever, amen.

Part of me—the shadow of teenage, virgin Hawk, who'd rubbed his dick raw just imagining Jack naked and couldn't have fathomed the things Jack and I got up to once we were naked *together*—still couldn't believe I was here, living the fucking dream.

But the truth was, life with Jack was so much more than anything I'd dreamed of.

It was goofy, spelled-out dad jokes and him knowing my favorite chicken marinade.

It was watching him evolve from reluctant cat owner to obsessed cat parent.

It was the library he'd built me and the Thin Mints he stashed there.

It was him embracing my maximalist decorating style and letting my collection of crocheted blankets consume our whole house.

It was "craft stuff" and "Hawk's books" line items in our budget every month without complaint, though we were supposed to be saving for our wedding.

It was the unexpected thrill of being the person who comforted Jack when he was sick or tired or disappointed.

It was him encouraging me to bring a needy ceramic

cookie jar into our home because I wanted it… and because *he* wanted me to have everything I wanted.

It was more than I'd known I *could* dream about.

It occurred to me, as I watched Jack snuggle a cat under each muscular arm so the "ladies" could look out the window —a thing he did regularly for these cats he'd once side-eyed —that it had been a really, really busy summer filled with important projects, and important work at the restaurant, and important shit to do at home… and I maybe hadn't taken the time to appreciate the most important person in my world. At least, not the way I should.

And suddenly, I couldn't wait another fucking minute to do just that.

"For fuck's sake. Why is it always Lydia?" Jack asked, interrupting my thoughts with a nod toward our smallest and most trouble-loving feline, who'd leaped up on the counter to bat at Sir Pecksworth, turning him so his beak faced the wall. "Does she need *more* stimulation, do you think?"

Without waiting for a reply, he shuffled the cats around in his arms until he could snag Lydia, too. Then he brought all five felines and their food out to the screened porch, where their water bowls and jungle gyms were already set up, and closed the door behind him.

"You really should have named that one Kitty," he said when he came back. "Even if a cat named Kitty *is* too on the nose. Kitty was the nicer Bennet sister. Instead, you named her after the sister who was an unmitigated pain in the ass, and now it's become a self-fulfilling prophesy. I'm warning you right now, if a cat militia comes to the neighborhood, I will not allow her to—"

"Jack," I interrupted. "I don't want to talk about the cats. Or *Pride and Prejudice*."

Jack blinked. "*You*? Don't want to talk about *Pride and Prejudice*?" He frowned. "Are you okay, baby? You do look kinda flushed. Are you thirsty? Or hungry?"

I wound my arms around his neck, pressed my body against his, and nodded. "Starving," I whispered, pulling him down for a kiss. "All of a sudden, I'm starving. But not for food."

Jack groaned, his hands sliding down to grip my hips and pull me closer, kissing me slow and deep. "Hawk—"

I broke off with a needy whine. "Need you. *Now*. Please, Jack."

Jack's eyes darkened, and his hands tightened on me with the kind of bruising intensity I knew, from personal experience, meant he was going to take me apart in the best possible way.

I barely had time to shiver before he was tugging off my T-shirt, skimming his callused fingers up my sides, tangling his hands in my hair, pushing me until my lower back hit the island.

"Here?" he asked, his voice rough as he trailed wet kisses down my neck.

"Oh yeah. Totally here," I confirmed, gasping when his teeth scraped my collarbone.

We'd had kitchen sex before. Like, a *lot* of kitchen sex. Christening this island and the marble countertops, the braided rug in front of the sink, and, on one memorable occasion, the door of the refrigerator (which had caused a messy but worthwhile ice-cube avalanche when my elbow had wedged against the dispenser).

But there was something different about this time. An intensity that hadn't been there in weeks… or possibly ever.

Maybe it was the heat. Maybe it was the realization that I'd missed spending quality time with Jack over the past few weeks. Maybe it was the happiness that fizzed like champagne bubbles under my skin every time I realized that Jack —the man I'd wanted since before it was legal—was now as dependable and necessary a part of my life as oxygen and didn't hesitate to show he felt the same way about me.

Whatever it was, it made my blood sing in my veins as Jack's hands made quick work of my jeans.

"God, you're beautiful, Hawk Sunday," he murmured, pulling back just slightly. His eyes roamed my body hungrily, reclaiming every single inch of me. Then he dropped to his knees on the hardwood floor.

The first touch of his mouth made me cry out, hands clutching the edge of the stone counter and head lolling back to rest against the upper cabinet. Jack had always known how to take me apart, but by now, he'd memorized every pressure point that made me tremble and the precise rhythm that drove me wild. He used that knowledge ruthlessly now… and I loved every damn minute.

"Jack." My legs trembled—literally, no kidding, trembled, like they might give out. "Inside me. Need you in me."

He pulled back, his lips shiny with spit and precum, his eyes wild. "You sure, baby? I was enjoying myself here."

The gravel-roughness of his voice sent a shudder of want through me.

"Very sure." I pulled him to his feet. "Hurry."

Jack chuckled as his hands fumbled with his belt. "So demanding, Hawkins."

"You love it," I countered.

"I love *you*," he corrected. Then, he lifted me up to sit on the counter and kissed me so hard I forgot my name.

"L-lube," I instructed a short time later. My breathing sounded like I'd been running marathons—plural—and I barely had the energy to wave a hand, but Jack knew exactly what I meant. I hadn't lived here a full week before Jack and I had realized the importance of keeping lube stashed all over the house.

He tore open the second drawer next to the oven and located the tube behind the measuring cups and spoons. His hand shook as he squeezed some out onto his fingers but steadied when he prepped me—gently but not too gently, just the way I liked it—his mouth never leaving mine.

When he finally pushed inside me, we both groaned and stilled for a minute. The physical burn, the fullness of it, was overwhelming. But the sensation of having him inside me, of being connected to him this way, was even more so.

"I missed you," I whispered, wrapping my legs around his thighs to draw him deeper. "Is that crazy?"

His expression softened. "If it is, I'm right there with you. I'm so fucking lucky. *We're* so lucky."

"You are the best thing in my world," I told him, meaning it.

Jack smiled. "You *are* my world," he said simply.

Then he started to move. The kitchen filled with the sounds of our breathing, with the staccato slap of skin against skin, with whispered endearments and little broken moans. The counter wasn't exactly built for comfort, but at that moment, I couldn't find one single fuck to give. The entire universe had narrowed down to Jack's hands, Jack's mouth, Jack's thrusts sending pleasure arcing up my spine.

His rhythm faltered as he got close, and his fingers dug into my thighs in a way I knew—and was fucking *thrilled* to know—would leave marks.

"Hawk," Jack gasped, pressing his forehead to mine. "I—"

"Yeah," I breathed. "Fuck yes. Come for me. Come *in* me."

His whole body tensed, and his face froze in an expression of ecstasy that bordered on pain, and then he came with a shout. Seeing him, *feeling* him pulsing hot inside me, sent my own release crashing over me like a tsunami.

After, we clung to each other, damp and breathless, like survivors of a peculiar kitchen shipwreck. Jack's heart pounded so hard I could feel it in my own chest.

"Holy shit," he finally managed, pulling back to look at me with glassy eyes. "That was…"

I nodded, just as dazed. We'd had some good sex. A *lot* of

great sex. Even some personal-record-phenomenal sex. This had been… something else entirely.

"And to think, I was tired when we got home," he murmured, nuzzling my cheek. "I think you inspire me, Hawk Sunday. Giving me all kinds of energy."

The word *energy* dropped between us, and I felt Jack go still. He pulled back, and we shared a single wide-eyed blink before he darted a lightning-fast glance at the counter where Pecky sat.

He laughed, but the sound was a little forced. "Jesus. I think the heat's fried my brain. Or, more likely, my hot fiancé has." He stepped back to help me off the counter, and once he'd made sure I was steady on my feet, he pressed a kiss to my temple. "Come shower with me."

"Definitely shower," I agreed, running a hand through my sweaty hair and feeling cum trickle down my thigh. I refused to look at the rooster. "I'm dirty."

"I like you that way." Jack grinned, taking my hand and leading me upstairs to our bathroom.

Under the cool spray of the shower, we took our time cleaning each other, our hands lingering on warm, soap-slicked skin. Because he smelled so good, tasted so good, *was* so good, I pressed a kiss to the underside of Jack's chin—my current favorite spot on his body. Jack growled and grabbed me around the waist, and the next thing I knew, I was pressed against the cool tile wall, Jack's mouth hot on mine.

I pulled back and laughed a little breathlessly. "Slow your roll, playa. I'm young, but even I need more than ten minutes to… to… *oh fuck,*" I groaned as Jack sank to the tiles and proved me a liar.

This time, the orgasms were slower but not one iota less intense. By the time I'd come down his throat and he'd spilled on the shower floor, we were both waterlogged, wrinkled, sated… and absolutely ravenous.

For *food.*

At least, I was pretty sure.

"I'm going to light the grill and make a salad, too," Jack declared, wrapping a towel around his waist and another around mine since I'd lost the ability to coordinate my movements. "And water. So much water."

"Yes. Hydration," I grunted. "Good."

I followed him back to the kitchen, watching a single droplet of water trail down the tanned column of his spine as he walked. I bit my lip and curled my hands into fists, fighting the urge to yank Jack's towel off his body and make love to him on the stairs.

Maybe it wasn't just food I was hungry for.

"Christ, I can barely keep myself upright," I croaked, mostly as a warning to my own wayward libido.

"Careful, baby." Jack frowned in concern. Once we got to the kitchen, Jack got me some ice water and insisted that I sit on the stool and watch him prep dinner… which didn't help matters. Jack moving around the kitchen, handling knives and tools with calm competence and focus, was and always had been one of the sexiest things I'd ever seen.

"You okay?" he asked once he had vegetables and chicken marinating in a bag on the counter. He came closer, stepping between my legs, and pressed a hand to my forehead. "You're still looking flushed. Think it could be heatstroke or something?"

I snorted, even as I leaned into the touch. "You think heatstroke's making me horny? Or that my hot fiancé is giving me heatstroke?"

Jack's eyes darkened. "You can't be horny right now," he said, even as his hands slid up my thighs and I noticed a growing tent in his own towel. "Impossible."

My body didn't seem to have gotten the memo about what was possible, though, because I was definitely horny— definitely *exceptionally* horny—even before Jack bit my jaw and sucked my earlobe into his mouth.

Later, after Jack had eaten me out and taken me again—on the kitchen floor this time—I found myself sprawled on the hardwood with my head pillowed on Jack's stomach. Every bone in my body felt spongy-soft, and my head felt like the unspun wool I'd gotten at the rummage sale earlier—fuzzy and amorphous.

"Wow," I slurred in the direction of the ceiling. "Just... just... wow."

"I want to make you food," Jack complained in a hoarse whisper, lifting one hand a couple of inches before letting it flop to the floor again. "But I can't reach it from here."

I snickered. "What the hell has gotten into us?" I demanded. "We're supposed to be an old, almost-married couple."

"Wellllll," Jack began in a teasing tone I recognized, "I know exactly what's gotten into *you*, Hawklet."

Despite my fatigue, I managed to roll over and tickle his ribs because I loved Jack too much to let him make silly jokes like that without immediate payback.

Jack grabbed my hands to stop me, and I pulled back just a little, full-on laughing now...

Then, I caught sight of the rooster on the counter and froze.

Sir Pecksworth sat exactly where I'd first put him... except I was almost positive I hadn't adjusted him after Lydia moved him. He definitely wasn't facing the wall now, though. In fact, his golden eyes seemed to stare directly at us, his ceramic beak tilted with something that almost looked like... avian satisfaction.

"Jack," I whispered.

He stilled beneath me immediately and followed my gaze, and then he froze, too. He cleared his throat. "The... the cat. Lydia. She must've moved him. Again. When we were upstairs."

I nodded. "Sure," I said faintly, though I knew—and I

knew *Jack* knew—the cats were on the porch and almost definitely hadn't evolved opposable thumbs and learned to open the door while we were upstairs.

"The rooster's just a decoration," Jack said firmly, though I wasn't sure which of us he was trying to convince. "The whole idea of him being sentient was a… was a joke."

"Yes," I agreed. "Obviously. He's adorable. And possibly lucky. A cock of good fortune, if you will. But he doesn't have, like, *powers*. He's just a… a cute piece of pottery."

"It's not like I need to be under the influence of a magical cock to crave you," Jack went on. "Or even to make love to you multiple times a day. It's not like this was unprecedented."

I nodded. He was right. It might not have happened in the past few weeks, but the potential was *always* there between us. A low-level hum in my blood, a banked fire that could turn into an inferno at the slightest provocation.

"You're everything to me. Always." Jack lifted his hand to push back the hair that had fallen over my forehead. "Even if I haven't done a very good job of showing that this summer."

Warmth unfurled in my chest, and I felt my smile soften. "We're a team, Jack Wyatt-almost-Sunday. That means there are going to be seasons where we have other stuff that's occupying our hours." I leaned in and pressed a kiss to his lips. "But I need you to know, no matter how busy we are, that you are my forever Mr. Darcy. The best man I know." I felt my smile go lopsided. "Maybe we needed the, ah, Cock of Good Fortune to remind us of just how lucky we already are?"

He made a thoughtful noise. "It might have been luck that we met in the first place, Hawk, but the way our relationship gets stronger every day, every year? That's because we both work to make it that way. Because no matter what, there will never come a time when you're not my first and last priority." His smile turned into a leer. "And I don't need the Cock of *Good Fortune* because I already have the only—"

"No," I said severely. I clapped my hand over Jack's mouth and absorbed his laughter into my skin. "Don't you dare make a stupid joke about my cock being enough for you."

"*That's* not a joke," he said, the words muffled by my hand. He grabbed my wrist and pulled my hand back to kiss my palm. "But it's kinda nice that you make the dad jokes *for* me, baby. I think this is how Knox must feel when Gage says something snarky."

I nuzzled back into Jack's neck. "Speaking of Gage and Knox... did you see them at the rummage sale earlier?"

Jack turned his head to give me better access. "Mmm. Sort of? Knox was helping at Betty Ann's table, and Gage was doing some kind of science booth for kids, I think? I didn't talk to them, though. They both seemed... distracted, I guess."

Grumpy was the word I would have used. Which was pretty much on brand for my brother but not at all for Gage, who was usually sunshine in a bottle.

"I saw Gage fast-walking through the crowd, and Knox called after him, but Gage pretended not to hear."

Jack laughed. "Can you blame him? Knox was probably sharing his thoughts on sock organization or some fascinating facts on lemur migration patterns he read about."

I poked my beloved in the ribs, and he squirmed. "I'm sure people say the same thing about me and my *Pride and Prejudice* retellings, and *you* seem to like them."

"No, I *love* them," he corrected. Then he shrugged. He pushed me back just slightly so he could cradle my chin in his hand. "You're not actually worried about Gage and Knox, are you? It was hot enough out there to make anyone short-tempered, but their relationship is solid. Besides, bickering is their foreplay."

I nodded. All of this was absolutely true. So I was

surprised to find myself blurting out, "But I feel like they need the Cock of Good Fortune."

Jack blinked. So did I.

"I… I don't know why I said that." I felt my face flush. "But it feels *right*, doesn't it? Gage loves quirky decorations, and… and Lydia clearly doesn't like Pecky," I reminded Jack solemnly. "She's already attacked him once, and it's only a matter of time before our murder feline finishes the job. So, really, it's for his own safety."

Jack tugged a lock of my hair. "Sure. Your brother's had a bad day, and you want to give him a possibly sentient sex rooster. That's reasonable."

I gaped at him. "N-nobody said *sex rooster*!" I protested. "Ew, Jack Wyatt! If anything, Pecky's a good luck charm!"

He grinned hugely, enjoying our teasing. "I think you mean a *get lucky* charm."

I tried to poke his ribs again, but Jack was too quick this time. He twisted so I was beneath him, the wooden floorboards cool against my naked back, one hand trapped in each of his as he loomed over me. I laughed breathlessly, half-annoyed and half-amused at how easily he'd pinned me.

Staring up at him, I saw everything I'd ever wanted reflected in Jack's blue eyes. The setting sun picked out the gold flecks around his irises and the gentle crinkles at the corners that deepened when he returned my smile, and I was struck for the million-billionth time by how ridiculously gorgeous this man was.

Jack's thumb traced along my collarbone—a barely there touch that made me shiver—and my pulse picked up. I saw Jack's eyes flare hot.

"I cannot wait to marry you this fall, Hawk Sunday," he said, his voice a deep growl. "I don't want to go a single day without that smile. I cannot wait to make it official."

My throat went tight. "It's like when Elizabeth Bennet said

she could not repress a smile at Darcy being so easily pleased," I teased in a whisper. "Just having you with me, knowing you love me, makes it hard not to smile."

"Then I promise to make you smile every day. Starting tomorrow, when I wake up next to my fiancé and help him rehome a possessed rooster cookie jar—"

I snort-laughed.

"—and ending... oh, seventy years from now, let's say, when I fall asleep next to my husband."

The sweet words, combined with Jack's weight pressing me to the floor, had a predictable effect... an effect that had nothing to do with roosters.

Jack noticed immediately and raised an eyebrow. "Reeeally? Four times in two hours, Hawk Sunday? That's gotta be some kind of record."

I grinned up at him unrepentantly. "Are you complaining?"

He shifted his hips, and I gasped. "Not even a little bit."

Much later, when we'd finally managed to eat dinner on the porch with the cats winding around our ankles, and I was sitting back in my chair with my legs thrown over one of Jack's strong thighs, I found myself glancing at Pecky, who sat on our kitchen counter like a poultry-shaped sentinel.

"I wonder what Pecky's story is," I mused. "How'd he get to be so... you know, *lucky*? And how'd a lucky rooster end up on a donation table at the Hookers' Rummage Sale?"

Jack's fingers traced up and down my knee idly. He glanced at the rooster, then gave me an amused look that said he still refused to believe in possessed ceramic poultry. But because he loved me, he didn't say that. "Sometimes things just end up where they're needed most," he said instead. "Whether it's a weird rooster finding its way to a rummage sale... or the most gorgeous, generous, loving human on the planet ending up in my arms." He brought my hand to his mouth and kissed my knuckles. "You're all the good luck I need, baby."

"Same," I whispered back, and I meant it with every fiber of my being. "Forever."

KNOX AND GAGE

CHAPTER THREE

KNOX

I woke up with a crick in my neck... and the sense that I'd made a grave tactical error somewhere along the line.

See, it turned out the sofa Gage and I had bought when we'd moved into the Pumpkin House four years ago was incredibly comfortable for watching movies and doing what Helena Fortnum might have called *canoodling*... but the fucker was not built for sleeping.

Not when you were over six feet tall.

Not when it was covered in squeaky, leathery material, *and* Little Pippin Hollow was being gripped by a heat wave, *and* you'd vetoed central air-conditioning during your remodel since it rarely got very hot in Vermont.

And especially not when you were supposed to be curled up beside the man you loved in your bed down the hall.

"Fuck," I groaned, rolling my shoulders as sweat already gathered at the back of my neck. Our house was an oven, and my phone claimed it was barely 9:00 a.m.

As I stared up at the ceiling, the previous day's events looped through my head... but made no more sense than they had the night before.

It had all started, I was pretty sure, when I'd gotten an

email from Rick, my former boss at Bormon Klein Jacovic, with an offer to consult on a short-term project in Boston. "Three months, Knox! Excellent pay, a chance to tackle something challenging, a no-brainer."

To my surprise, my first instinct hadn't been a hard no, but... well, *excitement*. Not for me—I'd already lived in Boston for years, seen all it had to offer, and quite literally had the T-shirt—but for Gage.

There'd been a time, right up until he'd come to the Hollow "temporarily" four years ago, when the man I loved had had an itch to do the big-city thing. And while I knew Gage wasn't exactly crying into his cornflakes these days, running his own app-development company from home for a bunch of clients who fucking adored him, with plenty of free time to run a volunteer computer science program at our nephew's school once a week, so that every kid in town knew his name and idolized him, it still niggled at me that Gage had never had the city experience he'd once craved.

I knew better than anyone that unfulfilled dreams could haunt a person. Sometimes you truly believed you were fine —resigned, reconciled, all that *adult* shit—when really you were ignoring and overriding. Eventually, you'd look up and realize you'd been missing out.

That's what had happened to me. I'd told myself I didn't need to live near my family, that I didn't want a romantic partner, that I was better off focusing on my career. Then Gage had come along, woken me up, and made me wonder what the fuck I'd been thinking.

I'd be damned if that happened to Gage. Not if I could help it. It was utterly unacceptable that the man who'd made all my dreams come true might have his own unfulfilled dreams ping-ponging around in the back of his weird and wonderful brain.

So, I'd emailed Rick back, asking him to send me the details, and once he had, I'd sat at the kitchen island and pored over his email while Gage had rushed around the house getting ready to run a robot-building demonstration for the kids who'd be attending the Little Pippin Hookers Rummage Sale.

I'd imagined what a sojourn in Boston might look like—me and Gage spending August weekends in P-town and soaking in the vibe of the place, strolling Castle Island and the North End, and watching the Head of the Charles Regatta. Like a vacation in slow-mo, just the two of us—because as far as I was concerned, it would always, forever, in all things, be the two of us.

And maybe, *maybe*, while we were there, I'd find just the right way to make our "always and forever" official and finally propose to the man. I'd brought up the subject of marriage once, just a couple of months after we'd gotten together, but even then, I'd known that Gage deserved a proposal that was bigger, splashier, and more memorable than a simple conversation. Nearly four years later, I still hadn't found the perfect time and place. *Yet.*

I'd been so excited I'd wanted to talk to Gage about the job offer right then and there, but once again, the timing was off. I didn't want to have a choppy, five-minute conversation while Gage was running around, and just as we were ready to leave, my brother Webb had called to say his husband, Luke, was in a tizzy, and could I pick up some things they'd forgotten at the farmhouse? And… well, long story short, I'd decided the subject of Boston could wait until later.

Except by the time later came… everything had gone pear-shaped somehow.

I'd been helping Betty Ann Wolff at the library table, hauling heavy boxes of books around, when she'd sighed. "Did you hear my grandson Charlie's moving to Arizona for his job, Knox?"

Since I was trying to be a more patient person these days, I'd nodded sympathetically while unpacking a stack of donated romance novels I'd swear had once belonged to my brother Hawk.

"I did hear. Big change, huh? But sometimes change is good, right?" I'd been thinking about my own life when I said it—about my finance career and the panic attacks that ended it, about Gage coming to town and remaking my life for the better, about the simple, elegant platinum ring that had been hidden behind the dress socks in my top drawer for ages. "I didn't use to believe that," I told Betty Ann, "but I've recently realized just how *necessary* change can be. Painful as it is, moving might be the best idea."

I'd heard a noise—a choky, coughing noise—and I'd glanced up to find my gorgeous boyfriend wearing faded cargo shorts, my old Hannabury T-shirt, and a look of mingled shock and disappointment. "You really think that?" Gage had whispered.

I hadn't known Gage and Charlie Woolf were close friends, so I'd been surprised that Gage was so torn up about it, but I'd shrugged and answered honestly. "In my experience, yes. You were the one who helped me see that, Goodman."

Gage had nodded once. Then he'd thumped a water bottle on the table, muttered, "Don't die of sunstroke, asshole," and stalked off.

This had been odd behavior, even for Goodman. One of my boyfriend's top three pastimes (along with eating dessert and having sex) was arguing with me, so he never flounced away when he was upset. And while he'd called me an asshole more than once—and I'd occasionally deserved it—it wasn't one of his usual endearments. Naturally, I'd called after him and tried to follow him, but he'd quickly gotten swallowed by the crowd.

I'd tried to chalk up this weirdness to the heat, which was making pretty much everyone in town cranky, and sure enough, he'd been much calmer by the time we'd gotten home. But when I'd tried to talk to him, he'd responded with distracted hums and nods—not a single dry, teasing comment or rolled eye to be found—which was when I'd gotten truly worried.

"Goodman," I'd said, drawing him into my arms once we'd gone to bed. "What's wrong?"

To my surprise, Gage had pulled away slightly. "Well, for starters, I'm hot and tired."

He'd sounded truly exhausted—and no wonder, between the heat and the exertion of the day—so I hadn't asked follow-up questions the way I usually did. "Right," I'd said. "Sleep, then, baby."

But worrying about him meant I hadn't been able to get to sleep, myself. It was a bit lowering to admit, but I, a man who'd gone decades without discussing his feelings, had forgotten how to compartmentalize in the four years I'd lived with someone who insisted on open, honest communication.

I'd lain awake beside Gage for hours before finally getting up, taking a cold shower, and flopping on the sofa in the living room so I wouldn't disturb him. I'd finally fallen asleep sometime after midnight, and now, for the first time in ages, I was waking up without Gage's flushed cheeks and bed head beside me.

I didn't like it one fucking bit.

The sound of the shower running meant Gage was awake, though, so I figured there was no time like the present to sort out whatever was bothering him. I levered myself off the sofa, headed to the kitchen, and had just gotten the coffee maker going when a knock at the back door startled me.

My youngest brother waved excitedly through the glass panel. Behind him, my soon-to-be brother-in-law wore a shit-eating grin while cradling something in a brown paper bag.

I threw open the door and stepped back with my arms crossed over my chest. "What?" I demanded by way of greeting.

"Always so polite and welcoming, Knox," Hawk said. "Might be my favorite thing about you." He narrowed his eyes and reached a hand toward my face. "Hey, why do you have weird creases on your cheek?"

I smacked at his hand and scowled. Figured the fucking sofa had left a mark.

"Hawk, it's not even nine o'clock on a Sunday morning, and it's five billionty degrees outside. Unless you've won the lottery—and I don't mean like the time Porter won a year's supply of pie; I'm talking enough cash money to fly us all to the Arctic Circle for an ice bath—I'm not in the mood for whatever you're peddling."

"Like golden sunshine," Hawk sighed happily. "Pure, unadulterated sunshine."

Despite the shitty sleepless night and the sweat rolling down my back, I found my lips twitching. I directed my next words to his fiancé. "I swear my brother didn't use to be this snarky. I blame you for this development, asshole."

Jack snickered. "Oh, no, he's always been exactly this—" He shot Hawk a look, then closed his mouth and shook his head. "You know, on second thought, I think I like my balls exactly where they are, and I'm going to ignore your statement." He hefted the paper bag a bit higher and stepped past me. "Now, where should we put your present?"

"Present?" I narrowed my eyes suspiciously as he set the object on the center island. "What for?"

"Because I'm a generous individual who finds joy in giving things to people I love. Obviously." Hawk's brown eyes blinked up at me innocently. Too innocently.

"Try again," I instructed.

"Jack and I found an amazing, whimsical antique at the rummage sale yesterday—"

Jack made a sound of disagreement, and Hawk shot him a look.

"Fine," Hawk said, "*I* found it. And I had a powerful urge

to bring it home. But then, upon… you know, *reflection*… I realized it wasn't meant for me. I was just a conduit." He looked solemn as a choir boy. "It's meant for you."

"Uh-huh. Because you see something whimsical and think 'Knox Sunday,'" I said blandly, folding my arms over my chest. "Who wouldn't?"

Hawk blushed. "No, see, it turns out it's kind of a… a lucky charm. A powerful one. Teagan Curran said so, and he's kind of a medium."

"A medium what?" I demanded.

"No, a medium, as in…" Hawk sighed. "Never mind. The point is, something told me I needed to bring it to you and Gage." He pursed his lips and looked pointedly at my cheek. "And that was *before* I realized you were sleeping on the sofa."

I could feel my own face going red. "I'm not—I didn't—" I broke off with a growl. I couldn't very well explain the situation with Goodman when I didn't understand it myself.

"Hmmm." Hawk gave Jack a look. "Sounds like we got here just in time." He tore the bag open and stood back with a flourish, as though presenting me with the holy grail. "I've got exactly what you need right here!"

I wrinkled my nose. "What the fuck is that thing?"

The supposed lucky charm was a gaudy-as-fuck ceramic rooster with a ridiculously puffed chest, one chipped wing, and garish red wattles that looked like a set of screaming red and engorged testicles attached to its weird chicken face.

It might have been funny, except that someone had also given the bird creepy golden eyes, and I swear, it seemed to be watching me.

"*He,*" Hawk corrected, giving the monstrosity a fond pat, "is not a '*that thing.*' He's Sir Pecksworth, the Cock of Good Fortune. Pecky, for short." He leaned toward me and confided, "He's magic." Then, straightening again, he added, "And he's also a cookie jar."

I blinked slowly, then frowned at Hawk in genuine concern. I knew the man enjoyed reading fiction quite a bit and had for years, but this was the first time I'd worried that it might be having a negative effect on his brain.

"Have you been reading outside again, Hawklet? Because one of the first signs of heatstroke—"

"Hush. I don't have heatstroke," Hawk said. "This rooster's genuinely lucky. Tell him, Jack."

Jack's mouth twisted like he was trying not to laugh. "I was already a lucky man, Knox... but I can definitely say that I got very, very, *very* lucky after that rooster came into my life." His eyes met Hawk's, and Hawk blushed. "But Hawk *might* be a little dehydrated."

Somehow, this made Hawk blush harder and bite his lip. Jack sucked in a sharp breath, and—

"Ugh. God. *Stop!*" I threw out a hand and made a retching noise. "The sex vibes in here are overpowering."

Hawk gasped. "Oh my God, it's working already!"

I had no idea what he was talking about, and I didn't want to know. My head was pounding from lack of caffeine, lack of sleep, and lack of *Gage*, which meant my patience was at an all-time low.

"Jack, if you're going to make horny eyes at my tiny baby brother, go do it in your own home, and stop defiling my kitchen with it," I said. "And take the weird rooster with you."

"He's not *weird*. He's handsome!" Hawk insisted. "Remember Uncle Drew had one just like this on the kitchen shelf when we were growing up?"

I gave the rooster a closer inspection. It *did* look sort of familiar. Maybe.

"I remember," I allowed. "He kept it right next to the Mason jar Porter painted at Scout camp, where Drew kept his marijuana stash."

"He painted the jar to say, '*Happy Mother's Day, Drew!*'" Hawk explained to Jack. "In glitter."

"Aw." Jack's face melted in a gooey frown. "That's really—"

I tightened my arms over my chest. "Irrelevant to absolutely anything?" I interrupted. "Yes. Yes, it is. I do not want your cock, so please take it and—"

"Whoa! Hey! Who's offering you cock?" Gage padded into the kitchen wearing nothing but a pair of athletic shorts—*my* athletic shorts—which hung indecently low on his hips. His hair was damp from the shower, his tan chest glistened with water droplets, and the second he stepped into the room, our eyes locked.

Despite everything—the blistering heat, yesterday's weirdness, *today's* weirdness—my mouth went dry at the sight of him. Four years on, he still affected me the way he had at the very beginning. *Mine*, a primitive part of me roared. *Mine, mine, mine.*

Gage tore his eyes away to greet Hawk and Jack, and I tried desperately not to stare at his naked abs.

"Morning, Gage!" Hawk smiled. "We brought you a housewarming gift. Surprise!"

"Uh. Okay." Gage frowned, confused. "But we've lived here almost four years."

"Which is why it's a surprise," Hawk said without missing a beat. He gestured proudly to the rooster. "This is Sir Pecksworth, the Cock of Good Fortune."

"I really wish you wouldn't call it that," I muttered.

Gage glanced at the ceramic chicken, and to my utter shock, instead of politely trying to hide his horror, his face broke into a genuine smile.

"Aw, what a cutie!" He moved closer, actually admiring the thing. "His eyes are so lifelike."

"Lifelike?" I sputtered. "Have you *seen* an actual chicken, Goodman? How can you be convinced that cows are out to kill you but say 'aw, cute' when presented with five pounds of homicidal intent covered in lead paint?" I thrust a hand toward the chicken, lost for words. "It's not cute. It's… it's…"

"A Cock of Good Fortune?" Jack supplied, trying not to laugh.

I glared. "No."

"I don't know," Gage said tightly. "I guess I have really questionable taste in what I find cute, don't I?"

I opened my mouth, then shut it again.

"I knew *you'd* appreciate him, Gage," Hawk went on. "I was just explaining to Knox that Pecky is all kinds of lucky—"

"Eh. Mostly *one* kind of lucky, to be honest," Jack murmured.

"—and that I feel like he's meant for you," Hawk finished.

"Too bad because Goodman and I don't want useless dust collectors," I said firmly.

Gage's head whipped toward me, and he set his hands on his hips—his nearly *naked* hips, given the dangerous way those shorts were riding down.

"Oh, *we* don't?" Gage tilted his head. "How do you know, Knox? How can either of us know how many dust catchers the other needs when we don't *talk* about it?"

I loved Gage's snark and—although I might pretend otherwise—his penchant for saying silly things. But this wasn't snark or silliness. There was a thread of worry and possibly hurt beneath his words that was absolutely unacceptable.

"Okay, that's it. Hawk, Jack, thanks for coming," I said. "Though I remind you that you weren't invited, and you really could have texted first. Now, grab your rooster and go. Goodman and I need to—"

"Oh, hell no." Gage grabbed the rooster and cradled it to his chest lovingly. "You're not getting rid of my Cock of Good Fortune, Knox Sunday. Hawk gave him to *me.*"

"Well, really, he's for both—" Hawk began.

Gage cut him off. "If you want to have a *discussion* about this, Knox, you let me know. But *I* think he's delightful and full of character, and *I* think he should sit on our mantel forever. And if you have a problem with that, you need to fucking express it."

He picked up the bird, crossed to the fireplace in five quick strides—shooting a glare at the disheveled sofa where I'd spent the night as he passed it—and set it in pride of place among the framed photos clustered atop it. Then he folded his arms over his chest, which only emphasized his bare torso.

I liked to think I was an intelligent man, generally speaking. Certainly, I was smart enough to keep my mouth shut, even though the fucking rooster was glaring at me over Gage's naked shoulder.

"Sure," I agreed. "Whatever you want."

"Whatever *I* want?" Gage fumed, casting his eyes to the ceiling. "See? This is exactly my point!"

Hawk shot me big eyes that screamed *Fix this, dumbass,* but how the fuck was I supposed to do that when I had no idea what was happening?

In four years together, nothing like this had ever happened to Gage and me.

I had no idea where this was coming from.

Hawk cleared his throat. "Well! Would you look at the time? We'd love to stay, but we need to get home right away so we can..." He hesitated and looked meaningfully at Jack.

"Er... deadhead the dahlias," Jack supplied.

Hawk looked like he really wanted to roll his eyes, but he nodded gamely. "Yes. Yes, it's a floral emergency. Gotta run." He grabbed Jack's hand and towed him toward the back door. "Anyway, enjoy your cock!"

"Stop calling it that!" I yelled just before they shut the door.

Jack muttered something under his breath that sounded like, "It's more accurate than you think."

Once they were gone, Gage and I stared at each other across the space. But Gage only held my gaze for a second before turning away to face that stupid fucking ceramic chicken.

"So… you slept out here last night, huh?" he said fake-casually.

"Honestly? I didn't sleep much at all." I took a cautious step toward him. "I knew you were upset. Angry, I guess? And I didn't know why. But I also knew you needed rest, so I didn't want to push the issue."

Gage huffed. "Didn't matter. I didn't sleep much anyway," he admitted. He blew out a breath. "I'm sorry, Knox. I was in a shitty mood. I'm still in a shitty mood, apparently."

I grasped his shoulders from behind. "Baby, will you please talk to me? I want to understand."

Gage's whole body shuddered as he let himself be pulled back against me, like he was as relieved by the contact as I was. "I know about Boston. About the job." He added quickly, "I wasn't spying, I swear. I went to print some stuff for the science booth from your laptop yesterday morning, and I saw the subject line of an email that said JOB OFFER and that it was from your old boss—"

"Hey. It's okay." I held him tighter. "I don't keep secrets from you, you know that." I ran my nose up and down the side of his neck. The scent of our bodywash on Goodman's skin settled something deep inside me. "I was waiting to talk to you about it when the time was right, that's all."

He turned in my arms, eyes stormy. "And when did you think would be the right time to tell me you wanted to move to Boston?"

"That *I* wanted to move?" I frowned, trying to follow his train of thought. "I didn't. I don't. I thought maybe *you* would. Short-term."

His eyes narrowed. "But… but… I don't understand," he admitted.

I shook him gently. "Next time you're *not spying*, baby, read the whole email. Rick's offering me a three-month project, starting in August. I thought you might enjoy a change of scenery. Or not." I shrugged. "Either way is fine with me, but—hold up. What did you think was happening here? That I was… moving away and leaving you behind?" I laughed, not because it was in any way funny, but because the idea was so absurd.

"No! Of course not." He placed his hands on my chest over my T-shirt and admitted, "In fact, my first thought when I saw the email was, *'Sorry, Rick, Knox and I are busy in Vermont, so you're shit out of luck.'*"

I half smiled. "Exactly."

"But then… then I heard you tell Betty Ann that change is necessary, and moving is the best idea, and I—"

I slid my hands up to cup his jaw. "The best idea for *Charlie*. We were talking about her grandson."

"I know! I got that. But the way you said it made me think." His fingers traced patterns through my shirt front that were highly distracting, though he didn't seem to realize what he was doing. "You used to have all these plans, Knox, I know you did. Career plans, travel plans. And you only came back to Little Pippin Hollow because Drew needed you—"

"And because I was having debilitating panic attacks," I reminded him wryly. "Let's not forget those."

"And then *I* came to the Hollow, and *we* got together—"

"Fell in love," I corrected softly. "One hundred percent, incontrovertibly."

Gage took a deep breath. "Yeah," he said softly. Then, more confidently, "Yeah, we did. But being in love with me doesn't mean all the other dreams you had went away. So, I started to worry that deep down, maybe you'd been missing out on other stuff because you know the Hollow is where *I* want to be. That I've been a selfish partner to you because it never even occurred to me to ask. And that you've been feeling some kind of way and thought you couldn't talk to me about it."

"Gage Goodman, that might be the silliest thing you've ever said," I informed him, conveniently ignoring that I'd had nearly the same worries about *his* unfulfilled dreams. "And I'll remind you that you once spent a six-hour road trip over-explaining the plot of every *Fast and Furious* movie to me, so you're clearing a high bar."

He scowled and tightened his fingers in my T-shirt. "If you're gonna pretend not to know why I say 'Hit the noz' when I speed up to pass a car, you can expect me to explain. *In detail.*"

I laughed. "I love you. I'm *in* love with you. You couldn't be selfish if you tried. And you're my best friend. I talk to you about everything."

"I know you love me. Of course I do. And I love you." He bit his lip. "It's just that sometimes we're having these amazing moments—like last summer during the fireworks and last Christmas when you dragged me on that amazing sunrise hike—and I think, 'Shit, I could *not* be happier right now,' and I look at you and... I feel like you're holding something back." He wrinkled his nose. "Okay, just hearing myself say that out loud, I know I sound ridiculous."

"Baby," I began, but then I wasn't sure what to say. He was right that I'd been holding back. Those moments he'd mentioned, it had been on the tip of my tongue to ask him to marry me, but it hadn't seemed quite right. Quite... special enough.

"Anyway, I guess I just want you to know that if you did want to move... to Boston or anywhere... I'd be sad for a minute, but I'd do it," Gage said firmly. "That's what I've been wrapping my brain around for the last twenty-four hours. I love our life here, but I love you more. And... basically, you're stuck with me, and I'm not letting you get away, so suck it up, buttercup, because this is your life now. Got it?"

The possessive edge in his voice made my heart race because he reminded me of... well, *me*, where he was concerned.

"You silver-tongued devil," I teased. "So romantic."

Gage wrapped his arms around my neck. "You like that, huh?"

"Mmm. It's like if a stalker wrote Hallmark cards."

He sighed. "My poetic genius is one of my best attributes and is sadly underappreciated around here."

"Oh, I appreciate all your attributes," I told him. I slid my hands down to cup his ass, which was firm and warm beneath the thin athletic shorts. "Some more than others."

He gave an outraged squawk that might have been convincing if you weren't close enough to see his teasing smirk or the heat kindling in his pretty, pretty blue eyes. Because I was, and because I could, I leaned in and kissed that smirk right off his mouth.

I'd intended it to be a quick kiss before we finished our conversation, but by the time I pulled back, we were both panting, and his eyes were unfocused.

"So... um. What were we talking about?" he asked breathlessly. His fingers crept up the back of my shirt.

I dipped my head and ran my tongue along the smooth, tan expanse where his neck met his shoulder. "Boston, I think? Something about that? I don't know."

"Right. Yes." He tilted his head to give me better access and rubbed his growing erection against my hip. "Fuck yes. Okay. We should... we should talk about that. Decide about that. Because if you... if you have dreams and... *fuck, yes, do that again...* and things you want to do in life... you tell me. Gage's Dream Fulfillment Service. Limited clientele, open 24/7."

There were all sorts of serious, mawkishly sentimental things

I could have—and would much later—say in response to a statement like that, but at the moment, I couldn't remember them.

"Come to think of it, there is one thing I want to do," I growled instead, cupping him through the thin fabric. "And I think it will be very fulfilling to me, personally."

"Yeah?" Gage's hand slid up to the back of my neck, pulling me closer. "Tell me all about it."

The invitation in his eyes was unmistakable, and I crushed my mouth to his, backing him against the wall beside the fireplace. His arms wound around my neck immediately, his body arching into mine like it had been more than a day and a half since I'd last fucked him.

Our kiss was a little bit desperate, a little bit relieved, and a whole lot devastating.

"Bedroom," he gasped between kisses.

But I shook my head. "Too far. Seizing this dream right here."

Gage's laughter turned into a moan, and he thunked his head back against the wall as I dropped to my knees. "Oh, fuck. What has gotten into you, boyfriend?"

"You," I said. One brief tug and his shorts surrendered to gravity. "It's always only you."

I took him into my mouth without preamble, loving the way he inhaled sharply and tangled his fingers in my hair. The salty, addictive taste of him, the breathy sounds he made, were familiar but more intense than usual, like every fucking sensation had been dialed up to eleven.

Apparently, a night on the couch was a powerful aphrodisiac.

"Fuck, Knox," he groaned above me. "I need… I need…"

I knew exactly what he needed—and didn't *that* make me feel ten feet tall, knowing I knew exactly what this beautiful man needed?—so I released him just long enough to retrieve the lube we kept in the side table drawer. Within seconds, I was on my knees again, working him open with my fingers and driving him crazy with my mouth until his abs were clenched and his thighs trembled.

"Oh, shit," he breathed. "Shit. Knox, please—"

I pulled off him just long enough to meet his gaze, the blue of his eyes so lust-bright it burned me. "You can take it, baby. Do it for me. Gage's dream fulfillment service, hmm?" I tapped his dick against my tongue, and he whimpered. "Don't come until I tell you."

I lowered my head again, taking him deep and swallowing around his length while he muttered curses and obscenities that only fueled me. Because one of *my* favorite pastimes was figuring out exactly how to make the man I loved come apart on my tongue, on my dick, and in my ass.

When I was satisfied that he was right on the edge, exactly where I wanted him, I rose to my feet. His eyes were glazed, his cheeks red, his chest sweaty, like he'd been fighting a hard battle.

"So good for me," I whispered, touching his cheek. Then I turned him and pushed his palms flat against the wall.

The sight of his tanned skin against the cream-colored paint he'd chosen when we'd first moved in—"*I don't know why it's called Milkmaid White, Knox, and do* not *make it weird, okay?*"—did things to my stomach. Things that were beyond lust, and wanting, and even beyond the love I'd felt for him all those years ago.

Gage was part of my soul now. The very best part. The fine, golden threads of him were woven so inextricably into the fabric of my family, my world, my *life*, that I couldn't pluck them out if I tried. He was it for me, forever. There would be no moving on, no matter what happened. And maybe I wasn't the best at telling him that in words—he was the serial-killer-poet of the two of us—so I needed him to know it now.

"I love you, Gage," I whispered as I lined myself up and pressed into him slowly. "Always. *Always.*"

"Yes," he hissed, pushing back against me. "God, yes."

Our style was usually playful and affectionate, with Gage sometimes laughing and teasing me until I came my brains out.

And that was perfect. *Usually.*

But right then, I knew neither of us was in the mood for that… which was fucking convenient since I didn't think I could have slowed down to save my life. Something primal was spurring me on, urging me to claim the fuck out of this man. My hands gripped his hips so hard I knew I'd leave bruises, and my mouth worried love bites into his shoulder and neck. *Mine, mine, mine, always.*

Based on the stream of nonsense coming out of Gage's mouth and the frenzied way he was working his dick, he was feeling the same.

"Harder. Just like… oh, fuck, Knox. Yes. *Yes.* Fuck. Own me. Fucking ruin me."

I was happy to oblige, driving into him with enough force to make everything on the mantel rattle. I wrapped one arm around his waist, knocking his hand out of the way, and found his cock hard and leaking. I gripped him firmly and stroked him the way he liked.

"C-close," he warned, bracing his forearms on the wall as his body locked. "So fucking close."

"Come for me," I gritted out. "Let me feel it."

Obedient for once, Gage came with a shout, his ass clenching my dick so hard that I couldn't hold back either. I clung to his waist as my vision went wonky, trusting him to keep us upright… or at least upright-ish.

We stayed like that for a long moment, locked together, chests heaving, my face buried in Gage's neck and his arms taking the brunt of our weight.

"Oh. My. Fuck," he slurred. "Am I dead? Holy shit, I am.

I'm dead. Damn. But you know, I'm okay with that. He died as he lived, thoroughly fucked."

I laughed, though it sounded a bit wheezy. Figured Gage couldn't go for long without teasing.

I carefully withdrew and turned him in my arms. "I love you. In case I didn't mention that."

"You did mention it." Gage kissed me and pulled back, his face flushed. "Several times. In fact, you might say it was pounded into me."

Laughing again, I admitted, "I don't know what came over me."

"Guess it's just my lucky day," Gage sighed.

Then he blinked, and his eyes met mine.

In unison, we turned our heads toward the mantel.

The fucking rooster stared back at us, his golden eyes glinting in the morning light. And I could've sworn—though I'd never admit it out loud—that the damn thing had moved to watch us.

"No," I said out loud.

But it was too late. Gage's eyes had widened and lit. "Oh my God! Is that what Hawk was talking about? All Jack's little get-lucky comments?"

"*No.*"

"The Cock of Good Fortune!" Gage crowed. "He specifically called it—"

"Goodman." I gripped his jaw. "I love you more than my life, but *we are not calling it that.*"

"Your brother gave us a sex chicken!" he said, delighted. "Is the fourth anniversary the Sex Chicken Anniversary? Way better than paper products."

I shook my head. "Gage, I do not need a sex chicken in order to fuck you, and I resent the implication—"

"Shhh. Don't offend him." Gage pushed his hand through my hair and held my hair back from my forehead. "I don't want to know what happens when the Cock of Good Fortune gets angry."

I rolled my eyes... but couldn't help giving the rooster a sidelong glance that had Gage cracking up again... and his sweaty, naked, delightfully messy body pressed against mine. My spent dick gave a hopeful twitch.

"We should probably finish talking about Boston," I said reluctantly, giving him a quick kiss. "Or not-Boston. I want to know what *you* want."

Gage smiled against my lips. "Boston can wait. What I want... is a nice shower and possibly a round two. With *you*, in case that wasn't clear." His grin widened. "Because you and me together, in any capacity, is my idea of perfection."

I stared at him for a long moment. Gage was right. Totally and completely right, as he so often was, though I didn't always admit it. Him and me... that *was* perfection.

And when I really thought about it... there was nothing more special than every fucking day that we spent together. So what the hell kind of perfect moment was I waiting for?

"Boston can wait," I confirmed, pulling him tightly against me. "But I'm warning you now, if you want a round two, we're turning the damn rooster around."

CHAPTER FOUR

GAGE

I FOUND MYSELF, sometime later that day, on the living room sofa, as late-afternoon sunlight streamed in the back window and Knox's arms were wrapped around me.

Ordinarily, this would be a good thing. The best thing.

Who the fuck didn't love sunshine? What dumbass would complain that the guy who'd starred in his lumberjack fantasies since long before they'd gotten together was sprawled on top of him? And who didn't want to be lying down, especially when they'd spent the whole night tossing in bed, and then had not one but two very athletic rounds of makeup sex with the man they loved?

Unfortunately, though, certain things about this setup were less than ideal.

For one thing, the sunshine had turned the living room into a furnace, and my whole body was glistening despite the fan perched on the coffee table blowing directly at us.

For another, a man with Knox's lumberjacky build was meant to be a mattress, not a weighted blanket. And for a third…

"This sofa is fucking killing me," I whimpered.

My human blanket chuckled and squirmed like he was getting more comfortable. "Funny, I was thinking it's actually much comfier now than it was last night." Knox kissed my bare shoulder. "Not sure why that might be."

I snorted and pushed at his chest. "Up, you behemoth. It's going to take me seventy-two hours to fully inflate after having you flatten me."

"Aw. Does that mean no round three?" he teased.

He rolled his hips, pushing our dicks together through the shorts we'd each thrown on after showering and, ah… finishing our other extracurricular shower activities. But when I felt the steel pipe in his pants, suddenly, I wondered if he was teasing.

"Wait, again? Oh, fuck," I said, arching into him. The stretch made my overused muscles ache in the best way.

"You're so easy, Goodman." Laughing triumphantly, Knox pushed himself up and flopped onto his side, squeezing his bulk between me and the back of the sofa, with his chest to my back and his arms around me.

Pretty soon, his breathing evened out like he'd fallen asleep.

I smiled. I was perhaps one degree Fahrenheit cooler in this position since one of Knox's long legs was still thrown over mine and his face was buried in my neck, but I didn't protest. In fact, I folded my arms over his arms to lock them in place because the past twenty-four hours had been a bit… well, unsettling.

Enough to make a guy justifiably clingy.

To be perfectly clear, when I'd seen that job offer email yesterday, I hadn't freaked out because I'd thought Knox would fuck off to Boston alone or force me to move either. My man wasn't just gorgeous, intelligent, invariably grumpy, and shockingly witty; he was also loyal as fuck. Specifically, loyal to me and my happiness. More than that, he was in love with me and didn't hesitate to show it.

We hadn't talked about marriage recently, but... who cared, really? Rings and certificates and ceremonies weren't a big deal when we were already each other's best friend and emergency contact and when both of our names were on the deed to our house.

Besides, I wasn't with Knox so I could have a wedding or a ring on my finger or any of that stuff. I was with Knox because I wanted to be with Knox, period. Saying I do in front of our friends and neighbors wouldn't change that one way or another.

In fact, if I'd ever stopped to think about it—and I hadn't—I'd have wanted us to keep doing what we'd been doing for the rest of our lives, albeit with a few more wrinkles and possibly some more nieces or nephews, if Webb and Luke ever stopped talking about it and got down to the business of giving Aiden siblings.

I mean, what more could a guy ask for, really?

I loved Little Pippin Hollow. I loved big family dinners with the Sundays, which rotated each week from house to house (or sometimes house to restaurant, when it was Jack and Hawk's turn to host).

Loved bitching with Helena Fortnum about the flatlander invasion every autumn, now that I was a local.

Loved that I got to witness Aiden morphing from a cute little boy into a scary-smart preteen attitude-monster who rolled his eyes at his dads but thought his Uncle Gage was hot shit.

Loved visiting Luke's classroom of second graders to do computer classes each week and watching their skills improve.

Loved that Knox made me coffee every morning using the fancy beast of an espresso machine we'd bought as a joint second anniversary present and which he'd promptly forbidden me to use because "All heroes need an Achilles' heel, Goodman, and the inability to brew drinkable espresso is yours."

Loved that we'd gotten into a routine of spending two weeks with my family in Whispering Key every January for "Second Christmas" and that Knox, who hated beaches, heat, and people in general, seemed to actually enjoy my dad's treasure-hunting stories and my brothers' teasing.

But when I'd spotted that email in Knox's inbox… well, it had made me wonder, you know? Like, how much of that life I loved was the future Knox wanted? He'd never said differently, sure… but I'd also never asked. And while I knew his happiness wasn't my responsibility, it was my priority because wanting the best for your partner was the gift-with-purchase that got dropped in your shopping cart when you fell in love.

So… what if he was prioritizing my happiness at the expense of his own?

Valid questions, maybe, but I was a little annoyed at myself for the way I'd reacted. After four years together, I knew that what made our relationship work wasn't some magical "happily ever after" juju but the fact that Knox and I were committed to making it work.

Falling in love with each other had been so easy as to seem inevitable, but being good partners to each other? That was a fuck of a lot trickier, especially since one of us was so cheerful he tended to repress things, and the other had anxiety that manifested as grumpiness.

TL;DR, I knew better than to take good communication for granted… and I'd still fucked up. It was a good lesson, I supposed, not to get complacent or take things for granted.

And to be honest, I couldn't be too upset at my overreaction… because Christ, that had been some amazing makeup sex.

Like, top-three-moments-to-replay-at-the-end-of-my-life sex.

And, cards on the table, I had a lot of sex to compare it to because Knox and I had a lot of sex.

As in… daily. Usually double-daily.

In all manner of positions, all over our house, and occasionally at other people's houses… or more specifically, in their orchards.

Once on a Whispering Key sand dune (ten out of ten for ambiance, zero out of ten for practicality because sand is fucking insidious).

Once in the back of a pickup truck at a campsite when visiting Knox's brother in western New York (seven out of ten for novelty, three out of ten for postcoital cuddles).

All of which was to say, I was a well-satisfied individual…

And still, I was fairly sure I'd been a virgin until this morning because that was how leveled-up our against-the-wall sex was.

I loved the rare moments when Knox lost a little bit of that urbane polish and got all growly, rough, and claim-y, but I'd never felt as thoroughly claimed as I had today.

I sighed happily.

Knox's fingers traced lacy patterns across my chest. "You're thinking awfully hard over there, Goodman." His voice was rough. "Pretty sure overthinking's my job in this partnership."

I snorted. "Not when I'm thinking about how well you fuck me," I retorted. "See, it'd be low-key arrogant if you were thinking about that." I glanced over my shoulder and caught Knox's green eyes. "Possibly even… dickish."

Knox chuckled, the vibration sending a bolt of heat straight to my cock. "Is it arrogance, though, if it's justified?" he mused.

"Obviousl—ohhh." Knox's hand clenched around my length, and the breath punched out of me. "Mmmpfh."

"Uh-huh. You know what I think? I think you like me dickish, Goodman. In fact, I think it's one of your favorite things about me," Knox whispered. His breath teased over my ear, and just like that, my whole body was on fire… again.

I would have blamed Hawk's sex rooster, but I knew better. This was all down to Knox Sunday, who'd lit me up this way for literal years.

"Would you like to know what I like best about you?" Knox's voice was rough, intimate in a way that made my heart skip.

"M-my devastating… wit?" I tried to sound casual, but the way his sure, knowing fingers stroked me kind of ruined the effect.

"That, too. But right now, I'm thinking about how you always surprise me." The fingers of his free hand found my nipple and circled it slowly. "Four years in, I sometimes still can't predict what you're going to say or do next. I fucking love that."

The simple words hit me hard. Knox was usually an acts-of-service guy more than a flowery-declarations guy, and when he changed it up like this, it killed me.

"Yeah?" I whispered. "Well, that's…" I swallowed. "That's…"

I couldn't complete the sentence. My brain cells were too busy cataloguing all the places we touched—Knox's scent in my nose, his arms caging me tight. His chest hair rasping against my back, his thick thigh wedged between mine. His hardening cock dragging over my ass, his fingers driving me crazy.

"And I love how responsive you are." His mouth found the sensitive spot behind my ear while his fingers pinched my nipple tight.

I let out a shuddering breath. My body was lighting up like a Christmas tree… as though Christmas hadn't already come twice today.

"I love how open you are with your emotions. How I never have to guess where I stand with you. You gave me your heart, Gage Goodman, and you've never once tried to take it back."

"Knox." I arched against him wantonly, blindly, proving the truth of his words, and the leather of the sofa creaked beneath us. I could feel every inch of Knox's cock as it slid between my cheeks and… fucking damn, it felt good. My own cock was throbbing in Knox's grip, leaking like a faucet.

"I love how generous you are," Knox continued relentlessly. "With your time, your friendship, your brilliant mind. You bring joy to every person in this town, and you never run out."

My throat went tight. I wanted to tell him to stop, but the other part was soaking up every sweet, perfect word.

How could you not be over-the-moon in love with a man who cared enough to know what you needed—even the things you didn't realize you needed—and make sure you got them?

Knox ground against me, and his cock caught on my rim, which was still loose from earlier. I pushed back, needing more.

His hand disappeared for a second as he levered up, reaching for the end table. Before I could utter a protest, his mouth was back at my ear, calming me.

"I've got you," he murmured, stroking lube-coated fingers over my hole, working them inside me. "Yeah. Fuck. Let me take care of you. I love how you trust me to take care of you, baby."

I inhaled a stinging breath through my nose. "Knox, I need… I need—"

"I know, baby," he whispered. Strong hands maneuvered me exactly where he wanted me—legs splayed wide, one knee hooked over his thigh—and then he slid inside me.

I cried out, overwhelmed, and not just by the physical pleasure. Knox spoke to me, held me, like I—snarky, happy-go-lucky, mildly cow-phobic Gage Goodman—was unbearably precious. Like I was the most important thing in his universe.

"Yesss," he groaned, setting a slow, deep rhythm that made kaleidoscope colors appear at the edges of my vision. "So good. How is it so fucking perfect, every fucking time?"

I wanted to say *because I love you, because you love me, because somehow, despite all the bullshit vagaries of life, our two slightly dented souls found their way to each other,* but unfortunately, all I managed was some high-pitched, inarticulate panting.

Still, I was pretty sure Knox understood.

Knox's fingers wrapped around my cock again. "I love your laugh," he said, his words tumbling over themselves in a rush. "Love how you make everything better just by being there. I love—" He broke off in a moan as I clenched around him.

"Please, Knox. Please," I begged, not sure what I was begging for—more, or less, or both at once.

"I've got you," he promised, fucking me harder, jerking me faster. "Always, Gage. Always."

My body bowed back *Alien*-style as my orgasm hit me like a freight train. I came with a cry that probably echoed around the Hollow and shot all over my chest... and quite possibly the couch. Knox's hands clamped around my hips hard enough to leave bruises as he thrust up into me once more and emptied himself inside me.

We collapsed like shipwreck survivors, both of us trembling, chests heaving, and absolutely soaked with sweat.

Seemingly out of nowhere, the sofa gave another plaintive squeal.

I laughed—well, as much as a person can when they still haven't caught their breath—and beneath me, I felt Knox's body shaking as well.

"You know," I said, my voice sounding a little bit drunk. "I think... maybe this sofa's not so bad."

"After today," Knox managed, giving the sofa a fond pat, "I'm having it bronzed."

I found myself grinning, though I wasn't sure how I had the strength. "A monument to commemorate my sexual prowess? I approve."

Knox's arms tightened around me, and he pressed a gentle kiss to the side of my head. "No, dumbass. A monument to commemorate our love."

I laughed again, wilder now. Definitely sex-drunk.

I couldn't think of a single thing in the entire universe better than this—being naked, filthy, and sweaty as fuck, sprawled on top of the man I loved. There was not a single career aspiration or far-flung adventure that would ever compare. All I wanted from the universe was more of this exact same thing. A whole forever of this. That was something worth commemorating.

I stopped laughing abruptly.

"Gage?" Knox asked, concerned. "Are you...?"

I wriggled slightly, and his softening cock fell out of me, making all kinds of mess. My sweaty limbs flailed a little as I tried to turn over, and Knox let out an ooof when my elbow slipped and wedged itself into his ribs.

"Sorry!" I said, reaching for his neck at the same time he tried to sit up. My hand met his face in the middle.

"Goodman!" Knox clapped a hand over his eye. "Are you trying to assault me? What in the—"

"Marry me, Knox!" I blurted. I grabbed him by the shoulders and held on tight. "I mean... I mean..."

I swallowed hard. Knox's eyes—well, the one eye that wasn't red and watery—went wide and shocked, which wasn't exactly encouraging. His hair was sweat-slicked and sticking up on one side, and I couldn't imagine what mine was doing, and I was pretty sure there'd be too much cum on the sofa to bronze it, assuming Knox hadn't been kidding about—

Focus, Gage. You got the man to fall in love with you. You can make this happen, too.

"Look, I know we haven't talked about it in a long time. Years. Several years, actually. And it's... it's okay with me if you don't want to anymore! I mean, obviously, people don't have to be married in order to be committed. And I know lots of people think marriage is heteronormative and... and... they don't need the government to sanction their partnership... and if you feel strongly about that, then I... I understand. But if you don't feel strongly either way, then... then I do. Feel strongly, I mean. About you. About us. About... getting married."

Knox stared at me like I was speaking some dialect of English he didn't know... which was silly since he'd learned to speak fluent Goodman years ago. But I couldn't turn back now, so I soldiered on.

"I didn't think I cared," I told him. As I perched in his lap, the fan blew on my sweaty skin, making me shiver. My fingers nervously carded Knox's messy hair back into place. "I didn't think I wanted the rings and the cake and the ceremony of it all. But I... I do. I want all of it. I want to stand up in front of our friends and families and promise to love you every day for the rest of our lives. I want to tell you, in front of the whole world, that I am yours, and I always will be. I want your ring on my finger because... well, because it's more convenient than carrying this couch around as a symbol of our love." I tried for a smile. "So, um. Will you, Edwin Knox Sunday, do me the honor of—"

Knox silenced me with a kiss, his lips crashing into mine with a kind of desperate intensity. When he pulled back a moment later, his eyes were shiny. And then, to my shock, he wrapped his arms around me, buried his face in my chest, and laughed so hard he made the sofa protest some more.

I blinked. "Uh. Baby?" I said after a moment. I put my arms around him and patted his back gently. "I'm not sure what's happening right now. This particular Knox-ian stress response is kind of hard to read. The tears are giving 'I'm trying to let you down gently'… or possibly 'My eye injury is worse than I let on'… but the laughter is—"

Knox lifted his head and cupped my chin in both of his hands. "Yes. Yes. Goodman. *Gage*. Of course I'll marry you."

It was only when I was able to suck in a full breath that I realized I hadn't been breathing normally. "Oh! Right. Good." I swallowed. "Wait, really?"

Knox's smile was brighter than the summer sun. "Yes, really. In fact—"

He stood quickly, nearly dumping me off the sofa and onto the rug before I scrambled to my feet. "Wait here," he said before running up the stairs.

"You're really giving a guy mixed messages," I called after him.

Knox thundered down the stairs seconds later, holding a small velvet box that made my heart stop completely. He skidded to a stop in front of me.

"I've had this for three years," he began. Then he opened the box to reveal a simple, elegant platinum band.

"Oh my God," I breathed. "Is this actually happening?"

"Yes. Finally." Knox's hands were shaking, which was more of a reality check than his words. Not even in my wildest dreams could I imagine Knox with shaky hands. "I've been waiting for the perfect moment to surprise you. Some grand, romantic gesture. The sunrise hike, the fireworks last summer… none of them felt right. Not special enough."

I winced. "Ah, shit. And then I come along and ask you the first moment it pops into my head, on a random Sunday, after acting like an asshole the day before, and when both of us are…" I gestured to my stomach, which was covered in cooling jizz and low-key starting to itch, and then to his crazy, sweat-mussed hair. "Ouch."

Knox laughed shakily even as he shook his head. He

cupped my jaw in one palm tenderly. "And then you came along," he agreed, "and reminded me that every day, every fucking moment, is perfect when I'm with you."

He dropped to one knee on the rug, right there by our unspeakably dirty sofa, and smiled up at me. "Gage Goodman, will you marry me? I want to spend all the rest of my moments with you, whether they're here, or in Boston, or anywhere else you ever want to go. I promise to make you coffee every morning—"

I sniffed a little but rolled my eyes. "Hardly an inducement since you don't trust me to use the machine."

Knox's smile widened. "And I promise to let you fill our house with..." He shot a glance at the mantel over my shoulder and curled his lip a little. "Weird, possibly sentient, decorative poultry that may or may not be trying to murder me through an overabundance of sex."

"Hey!" I laughed a little. "No such thing. And no dissing the Cock of Good Fortune, or all bets are off!"

"And I promise to love you... every perfect, ordinary day... for the rest of our lives."

"Well, when you put it that way." My eyes were distinctly leaky, and my vision was blurry, but Knox's hand on mine anchored me, as usual. "Yes, I will. Fuck, I love you."

Knox snorted a little as he lifted the ring from the box and slid it onto my finger. It fit exactly right, because of course Knox had made sure it would.

"I love you, Gage Goodman," he said solemnly. Then he tugged my hand until I was kneeling on the rug beside him and kissed me until we were both breathless for the fourth time that day.

"Just remember," I told him later, when my head was nestled on his shoulder and I'd lifted my hand so the dying sunshine struck bright sparks off the metal. "Who asked who first."

It was a sign of just how tired—and, okay, blissfully happy —Knox was that he didn't even argue.

"You've been surprising me since day one," he said. "Frankly, I should have anticipated that you'd surprise me in this, too." He pulled back and gave me a mock glare. "But don't try surprising me with a wedding, understand? I want something gaudy as fuck. White doves, prissy wedding colors, the whole nine."

I snorted. "Maybe next summer, in the orchard. No doves, just apples. And the cows can watch… but only if they maintain a respectful distance."

He laughed… then yawned. "Deal."

"And in the meantime…" I hesitated. "Maybe… Boston? I think I might like it. Temporarily. As long as we're back in plenty of time for Hawk and Jack's wedding." I frowned. "Unless you think they'll need our help?"

Knox closed his eyes and laughed sleepily. "Hawk's been planning his wedding since he was four, I think. He'll be fine without us. Besides, Webb and Luke are here. Assuming they haven't combusted from stress by then."

I made a considering noise. Webb had been wound tighter than a spring lately, which wasn't totally off brand for him. But these days, his normally easygoing, laid-back husband was getting in on the act.

"Luke nearly bit my head off yesterday at the science booth," I told Knox. "And then apologized profusely a second later, but still." I traced a finger up Knox's chest. "Do you know what's going on?"

Knox's shrug made my head bob up and down. "Webb loves sharing his deep feelings with me about as much as he ever has. If I had to guess, I think it's about them having a baby."

I nodded. Webb and Luke had first talked about having a brother or sister for Aiden nearly as long ago as Knox had first mentioned marriage to me. But as far as I knew, they hadn't done anything about it. "Do you think they need money? Because we could—"

"I offered once before," Knox admitted. "A few years ago. Webb said he had it covered. You know how stubborn he can be." He shrugged again, but I noticed that his eyes were open now and thoughtful. "He and Luke will work things out. They love each other too much not to. Just think how much those bugle-blowing fools have overcome already."

"I know. I wish we could help, that's all." I held my ring up again. "I'm pretty fucking happy right now. I want all my people to be happy, too."

"I know." Knox kissed the top of my head. "But without a magic wand, I'm not sure we can conjure them up a baby."

I froze. "Knox. I don't have a magic wand, but I do have a possibly magic rooster..."

"Goodman," Knox groaned. "Baby. No. You really don't."

"But you said yourself that Pecky inspired you," I reminded him.

"I don't care how inspiring your sex chicken is. Webb can't get Luke pregnant!"

"Pecky's not a sex chicken," I said reproachfully. "He's the Cock of Good Fortune. He makes dreams come true."

Knox opened his mouth to protest further, but I waved the ring on my left hand in his face—all the evidence I needed, really—and he shut his mouth with a clack.

"You're seriously suggesting we pass the sex rooster to Luke and Webb?" he asked instead.

"Yes. Or, if you'd prefer..." I laid my head back down on my boyfr—my *fiancé's*—shoulder. "Pecky could stay on our mantel and keep an eye on us permanently."

I didn't have to turn my head to know that Knox had opened his eyes and glared at Pecky... or that he'd noticed Pecky's golden eyes positively glowing in the setting sun.

"On second thought," Knox said a moment later. "You might have a point."

"Uh-huh." I grinned. "Stick with me, Sunday. I have all the best ideas."

I did turn my head then and found Knox watching me, his green eyes soft and crinkled at the corners.

"I'll stick with you, Gage Goodman," Knox vowed softly. "Always."

LUKE AND WEBB

CHAPTER FIVE

LUKE

I OPENED the back of my SUV and heaved a sigh at the mound of groceries there, which seemed to have doubled during my two-hour drive home.

"'Move to Vermont,' they said," I muttered under my breath as I grabbed a cooler filled with frozen food. "'Enjoy rural living,' they said. Nobody talks about how far it is to Costco."

A deep chuckle emerged from the barn, and I turned to find my husband with one boot propped back against the siding, thickly muscled arms crossed over his equally muscled chest, watching me with a smirk.

"Hey, gorgeous," he said softly. He curled his fingers in a come-hither gesture. "C'mere and kiss me."

I rolled my eyes. Webb's hair was damp with sweat, his legs and boots coated in flecks of grass clippings, his blue T-shirt and jeans streaked with substances I couldn't immediately identify... and probably shouldn't try to. But his eyes were filled with the same absurd level of affection, adoration, and lust as they'd been during our weird, wonderful, ass-backward courtship. Three and a half years after drunkenly blowing a bugle and finding ourselves hand-fasted—three and a half years of mostly joy and occasionally heartbreak—Webb Sunday still made my heart stutter.

So of course, I did as he requested, dropping my box of groceries and sauntering toward him… but *slowly*, pretending to play it cool.

I failed miserably, if the way Webb's smirk grew was any indication.

When I got close, he lifted a hand—probably the only part of him that had been recently washed, I noticed with amusement—to grip my chin. Then he lowered his lips to mine and kissed me, hard and deep and claiming, until my toes curled inside my sneakers.

Ask anyone in Little Pippin Hollow, and they'd tell you Webb Sunday was kind of a Renaissance man. A business owner, an heirloom orchardist, an amazing father, a Scout volunteer, a brother who'd do anything for his siblings, a pillar of the community.

But what I knew—and what no one else around here would ever learn, if I had anything to say about it—was that Webb's greatest talent was *kissing*.

Webb kissed me like I was his sole focus, like he had all the time in the world and planned to spend every second of it imprinting his love for me right into my bones.

So it was zero surprise that I forgot all about my long drive, about The Big Conversation I knew Webb and I needed to have, about the popsicles dying a slow, sticky death in the cooler. I sucked in a big lungful of cut grass and clean sweat and chased the taste of Blue Raspberry Gatorade—Webb's summertime hydration of choice—with my tongue.

Sometime later, Webb pulled back just far enough to press our foreheads together. "Mmm. Missed you," he murmured.

I huffed out a laugh, still breathless and swamped by love. "Since you got out of bed this morning?"

"Morning comes early in summer, baby. You know that."

I nodded. Webb was out of bed with the birds, especially

when it was forecast to be beastly hot, as it had been for the past week…

And *especially*-especially when staying in bed meant a greater-than-zero chance of me forcing him to have The Big Conversation.

"Besides," he continued, setting his hands on my hips and giving me a smile full of *intent*. "I knew you were dropping Aiden and the dog at Porter and Theo's place—"

"Porter was already hauling out his 'Special Effects for Beginners' kit when I left them this morning," I interrupted. "He and Aiden are going to build a working volcano, recreate a battle from *Return of the King*, and make hot fudge from scratch."

Webb shook his head. "God help the professor."

"Nah, Theo looked suspiciously excited. Pretty sure your brother's letting him be Gandalf." I grinned broadly. "Your family's the best."

Webb's green eyes flared hotter as he tracked my smile. "They are. But they're also always fucking *here*." His fingers tightened on my hips. "Tonight, though, Aiden and Bear are gone, Em's visiting her college friend, and your mom and Aunt Sue are still on their Irish wool tour. You know what that means?"

I pretended to think about it. "There's a possibility the pint of ice cream I put in the freezer yesterday isn't empty and that I'll be able to crochet more than two rows of my temperature blanket while we talk without interruption?"

He wrinkled his nose. "Sadly, no. I caught Aiden shutting the freezer guiltily last night and smelling distinctly like Boston Cream Pie. But!" He pulled me against him. "It means we're alone. *Truly* alone. And I'm thinking we can find something way more fun than crocheting to do."

I noticed he didn't mention anything about *talking*.

"More fun than crocheting?" I ran a hand over his chest,

his hard muscles warm under my hand. "I don't know. I really like crocheting."

"Uh-huh. But it's been nearly a week since you and I… blew a bugle." He bounced his eyebrows lasciviously. "And evidence suggests you like that, too."

I snorted. Webb was hot *always*, but when he gave me that wolfish grin and let me see the goofy side of himself he hid from most people? I was a goner.

He was right, too, that it had been a week since we'd gotten any action. Of course, the reasons for this were less about us finding time alone and more about Webb avoiding The Big Conversation… but when that teasing smile was shining down on me, making my heart race, I didn't want to quibble.

"Well, you're in luck, Mr. Sunday. I happen to find myself in a bugle-blowing mood." I knew I sounded utterly besotted, and I didn't care one bit. I rubbed a smudge of dirt off Webb's cheek with my thumb. "Have you been wrestling the tomato vines in my garden with your bare hands again?"

"Not today. I was down with the sheep most of the afternoon. I'd planned to get cleaned up and start a seductive dinner before you got back, but Tater rolled herself straight into a thistle patch again, and Prissy decided to use my distraction to cover her jailbreak."

I groaned. This was all too familiar. "Please tell me you caught her before she got to the road."

"Caught her *in* the orchard, actually. I assume she was excited to check the Black Oxford grafts." He winked. "But it took a while to get her back in her pen, so I only got back a minute before you did."

"Just in time to help me put the groceries away." I tilted my head toward the open trunk and fluttered my eyelashes. "You know, it's a scientific fact that grocery carrying begets bugle blowing, husband. In case that matters at all."

"That so?" Webb looked like he was fighting laughter.

"And all this time, I thought old Ernie Spencer at the grocery store was just being *nice* when he asked if I needed help with my bags."

I poked my husband in the ribs, then grabbed his hand and towed him, laughing, toward the trunk. But the grocery explosion waiting there sobered him up real quick. "Jesus fuck, baby. I thought we were having just a *family* cookout tomorrow night, not inviting half the town."

"Yeah, well. It feels like our family *is* half the town." I rubbed the back of my neck. "Besides, it's not all ours. You know how it is. You tell one person in the Hollow you're going to the big store, and suddenly, sixteen other folks are texting to ask if you could grab them just *one tiny thing* that Peebles Market doesn't carry. Before you know it, you're filling two carts, and most of it isn't even yours."

"You say that, but I know these industrial-sized boxes of granola bars have Aiden's name all over them." Webb hefted a double stack of groceries, including the bars.

"True." I laughed as I picked up the cooler of frozen stuff and followed Webb around back to the kitchen door. "Along with the dozen frozen pizzas and the high-protein oatmeal he asked me to get."

"High protein? Since when? Doesn't he like the kind with high-sugar and candy pieces in it?"

"Seems our boy's got his sights set on making the travel baseball team next spring. I got a whole earful about it on our drive to Porter's today. And I'm not saying that's directly related to Hannah Melo thinking baseball players are the coolest… but I'm also not saying it's *unrelated*."

Webb stopped walking and turned to blink at me. "No way. Aiden doesn't have crushes. He's still a little kid. He's only—"

"Ten?" I said, mock sadly. "Yes, with the appetite of three grown Sundays, a snarky preteen attitude courtesy of his Uncle Gage, and a penchant for calling both of us *bruh*. He's growing up whether we like it or not." I summoned a smile. "But, hey, no need for us to get nostalgic just yet, right? Not when we'll be drowning in diapers by the time baseball season starts."

Webb resumed his walk with a grunting noise that could have meant anything. Possibly, *I stubbed my toe.* Potentially, *Yes, but Aiden's relentless progress toward adulthood is a reminder of my own advancing age, and I'm having an existential crisis.*

But since I knew my husband, knew all his best and worst traits, knew every freckle on his shoulders and every worry in his heart, I knew this grunt meant *I'm terrified we'll be disappointed by our most recent attempt at surrogacy again, so I get weird every time the subject comes up.*

My chest squeezed a little.

Because I was ever hopeful, though, I kept my smile firmly in place as I followed him up the porch stairs. "Speaking of our babies," I said brightly. "Did you see the ultrasound pics Josie sent yet? The twins don't look like blobs anymore. They look like actual, miniature humans with these tiny little fingers and noses. And I know we decided, before we started surrogacy, that we weren't going to find out who fathered each of them, but I swear to God, Baby A has your exact profile. Wait until you see the pic—"

"Fucking Christ!" Webb exploded.

I stopped in my tracks, my smile fading. "Webb—"

"Sorry, baby. That wasn't about you or… anything," Webb said, instantly contrite. "I can't see around these boxes, and I nearly tripped over a—" He lifted the groceries higher so he could peer down at the spot beside his boots. "Ceramic chicken?"

I set the cooler down on the porch and found that there was, indeed, a white ceramic chicken blocking the door, with a bright pink sticky note stuck to its head.

As Webb went inside, I grabbed the note and read aloud. "*Dear Webb and Luke. Congratulations! You are now the proud owners of Sir Pecksworth, aka Pecky, aka the Cock of Good Fortune (though Knox says not to call it that where he can hear you). Hawk passed this magical cock to us, and we got very lucky as a result—"* I glanced up. "The, ah, *very* is underlined. Twice."

"Jesus," Webb muttered, lip curling.

"We got very lucky as a result," I repeated, *"which we'll tell you all about tomorrow night at dinner—"*

"They fucking will not."

"—so we're passing him on to you. Give Pecky a good home, and his luck will be yours. Love, Gage and Knox."

Webb shook his head. "My brothers get weirder with each passing day."

He wasn't wrong. Still…

"It was sweet of them to think of us, though, right?" I picked up the rooster for a closer look and pulled up its hinged lid. "Oh, and it can hold cookies!"

"Hmm." Webb peered over my shoulder at the rooster. "You know, when Drew lived here while we were growing up, he used to have a whole lineup of ceramic poultry on that kitchen shelf." He pointed at the shelf over the counter, which now held my hand-thrown mixing bowls. "Ducks with come-hither eyes, chickens with lipstick painted on, geese with dapper blue bow ties. And he used to hide his weed stash in a little jar right behind them—" He stopped as if he'd heard his own words, and amused green eyes met mine. "This is the first time I'm realizing those things might be related."

I laughed out loud. "Well, I think Pecky's kind of cute." I ran a finger over his chipped wing. "And, ah, extremely well-endowed in the wattle department."

"Bulging wattles like those are a sign of heatstroke in roosters," Webb informed me seriously.

I felt a burst of fondness for my husband. "Heatstroke might explain his trippy eyes, too. But he's got personality." I set the rooster on the sideboard near the front hall, where he'd be safer next time Aiden *"accidentally forgot, bruh!"* that he wasn't supposed to practice baseball indoors, and turned back to my husband. "So! About those ultrasound pictures. Wanna see—?"

"Later. I'd better get these groceries in before they melt," Webb interrupted. "You start putting stuff away, and I'll grab what's left in the car, okay?"

"Yeah," I said faintly, though Webb had already fled. "Sure."

I blew out a breath and let my neck fall back, inspecting the ceiling beams for extra patience, but there was none to be found.

It wasn't that I didn't understand why it wasn't easy for Webb to talk about this. Why he was cautious. Hell, why he was downright scared. After all, this wasn't our first or even second surrogacy rodeo.

The first time around, we'd been nothing *but* optimistic. The minute we'd found a surrogate, Webb had started working on a handmade crib, I'd started crocheting things for the nursery, and we'd debated how we'd announce the eventual pregnancy. When our surrogate had changed her mind late in the process, sending us back to square one, the disappointment had been crushing.

The second time around, we'd tried to keep a leash on our expectations to protect ourselves from disappointment, but we'd both done a shit job of it. Month after month, we'd held our breath, but when our new surrogate hadn't gotten pregnant, our hearts had broken all over again.

Coming up with the money and the heart to try again had been... well, fraught. Webb had openly questioned whether we should give up, and I'd been on the fence, myself. But when a popular knitwear designer had asked to buy the rights to one of my patterns for an exorbitant fee—more than I'd made on *all* my other patterns put together and almost exactly the amount we needed—it had felt like fate. I'd pleaded with Webb to give it just one more shot, and he'd agreed.

This time, though, Webb wasn't just tempering his expectations; it was like he was willfully preventing himself from getting excited. Even though Josie had gotten a positive pregnancy test. Even though she was four months along already with our twins.

When I climbed into bed at night and shared my own excitement about our girls, or Josie's newest pregnancy symptom, Webb would give me a vague, supportive smile... while his eyes swam with anxiety. And as soon as I finished talking, he'd jump up, muttering something about feeding the dog, or cows, or sheep, and flee the room.

Anytime we curled up together on the sofa, Webb would listen attentively to *my* plans for the nursery and *my* ideas for baby names, but when I asked what *he* wanted, he'd feel the sudden, immediate need for a shower, a snack, or a trip to the basement to triple-check that he'd turned the lights off.

He was clearly trying to be a supportive husband and father, as usual, and I knew how committed he was to our family. That never changed. But I hated how his anxiety was creating literal and figurative space between us.

I'd been as patient as I could, but it was past time for us to have The Big Conversation about what was going on with him and how we could work through it together.

Webb hauled in the last of the groceries and ran a hand over his sweaty hair. "Need my help putting things away? 'Cause if not, I could really use a shower, and then we can do... well, anything you want." His sweet, sexy grin was back.

It was on the tip of my tongue to ask if "anything" involved telling our loved ones about the twins' existence sometime before they graduated college, for fuck's sake, but I bit my tongue.

Webb swallowed, obviously sensing my mood, and hesitated. "Luke, I..." He broke off with a shake of his head.

I loved Webb Sunday. Loved him more than anyone on Earth. And I didn't want to fight with him. Heck, I wasn't even *angry*, really. What I wanted was to make this weird barrier disappear so I could feel close to my husband again. For him to let me in and explain what he was feeling. I knew fighting wouldn't achieve that.

"Go on," I said, shooing him with my hand. "Get clean."

I watched him go, and a moment later, I heard the water turn on in the big downstairs bathroom, where we usually cleaned up after farm chores. With a sigh, I turned back to the groceries... but my eye caught on the cute little rooster, who seemed to be watching me.

"Hey, if you're as lucky as Gage says, Sir Pecksworth, I could use a little help," I said out loud, and then my whole face got hot.

Was I honest to God talking to Gage's lust-inducing cookie jar? Was this what I'd sunk to?

As I packed and sorted the rest of the groceries, I considered how best to start The Big Conversation, but I kept getting distracted. The sound of water splashing against the shower tiles floated through the half-open bathroom door, mingled with Webb's soft, unconscious sighs as his muscles relaxed beneath the spray. It didn't help that I could picture what was happening in the bathroom exactly—Webb's tan skin glistening, the water turning his long, dark eyelashes into spikes, his muscles flexing as he soaped himself everywhere.

I bit my lip and flushed, instantly aroused. Meanwhile, a voice in my head that I didn't recognize said, *If you want to feel close to your husband, Luke... what the fuck are you doing all the way out here?*

The voice made a damn good point.

Already half-hard, I stripped my shirt off and padded toward the bathroom.

Webb stood facing the spray, much the way I'd imagined him. His chin was tipped to his chest, his eyes closed, his hands braced on the wall, as water coursed down his spine and over the firm curve of his ass. Steam curled around every bump and ridge of muscle, from the sharp cut of his biceps to the narrow taper of his waist.

He was so fucking strong, this husband of mine. So used to carrying things—whether it was sheep or groceries, the weight of his family's needs or his own fears—on those broad shoulders. But the man needed to remember that he didn't need to carry things on his own. Not while I was around.

As I watched, Webb arched his back, stretching his muscles, and let out a long, low groan. His fingers flexed against the wall, including the one with the simple titanium wedding band that matched my own, and just like that, my mouth went dry, and my cock filled.

It hit me in the gut then that this man was *mine*. Mine to touch. Mine to rely on. Mine to protect. Mine to love, even— or *especially*—when he was terrified and putting roadblocks between us.

I stepped into the room, quietly stripping off the rest of my clothes as I went, leaving a trail like breadcrumbs across the black-and-white tiles.

Webb startled and turned as he heard me approach, but when I opened the glass door and stepped into the shower with him, his expression sharpened to something that made anticipation curl in my belly. My knees went weak… so I dropped to them.

He gasped in surprise, quickly positioning himself so that his big body blocked most of the shower spray, and I smiled softly. Then I wrapped a hand around the base of his cock and leaned in, nuzzling my face into his hip, dragging my nose along his length, just breathing him in.

The clean pine fragrance of Webb's soap combined with the musky salt of his skin wasn't just hot as fuck, it was like a trip wire in my brain—a key in a lock that sent all my barriers and inhibitions crashing down. This was safety, this was home, this was *Webb*. The way Webb hardened in my hand at just that bare touch showed he felt the same. And when his strong fingers twined through my hair and I glanced up, the look in Webb's eyes—the open, naked hunger there—made my belly flip.

Wordlessly, I took him in my mouth, groaning as my lips stretched around him and his familiar taste hit my tongue. Webb's breath punched out of him on a gasp, and one of his big hands flew to the tile wall to steady himself while the other tightened painfully in my hair. I licked and sucked him with feverish absorption while my free hand moved lower, rolling and cupping his balls, tracing his rim with wet fingers.

With no lube in this bathroom—one downside of having a curious preteen *and* Webb's sister home on summer break was that we didn't get to turn every nook and cranny of our house into a lube cubby like my brothers-in-law did—I wouldn't go much further, but Webb let out a low moan and spread his legs in invitation anyway, willing to take whatever I'd give him, trusting that I'd make it good.

I didn't hold back, using my tongue and fingers in the precise way I knew would take Webb apart, wanting every flick of my tongue, every press of my fingers, to send a message. *I see you. I love you. I'm here, and I'm not letting go.*

Webb's big thighs trembled, his hips stuttered, he shouted my name so loud it rang in the small space, and he came down my throat with his hand still fisted in my hair like he couldn't bear to let me go.

Before I'd caught my breath, Webb grabbed me under the armpits, dragged me to my feet, propped me against the far wall, and sank to his knees.

"Webb." The word was half sigh, half plea, my cock already so hard it ached.

He didn't answer with words, just held my hips in place as he pressed open-mouthed kisses along the inside of my thighs, and his beard rasped gently against my skin. When he tongued the crease of my thigh, my breath hitched. When he licked a hot, wet stripe up my cock, I gasped, arching back against the cool tile.

If Webb's kisses made me feel like his sole focus, the way he made love to me made me feel like a god—not a feeling I'd ever had before him. His mouth closed around me with aching slowness, sucking me deep, then shallow, using his tongue to tease the tip until I whimpered. Every move was deliberate. Relentless. Worshipful. Like he was savoring every inch, every taste of me, and couldn't get enough. Like the only thing that mattered in the universe was my pleasure.

My head thunked back against the tiles as his hands were suddenly everywhere—cupping my ass, spreading me open, stroking along my ribs like he wanted to memorize my shape. The contrast of that hot mouth and those big, roving hands had my muscles quaking and tears leaking from my eyes. There was nothing better than the way Webb loved me. Not one single thing.

I came so hard my vision whited out and my knees threatened to buckle, but Webb's hands were back on my hips, holding me up... because that was what we did for each other.

When I finally blinked my eyes open, dazed and boneless, Webb rose to his feet. "I love you, Luke Sunday," he said, voice wrecked, like he thought his actions might not have been convincing enough.

I wanted to get up on my tiptoes and kiss him, but my muscles wouldn't cooperate. Instead, I let my head fall against his broad chest, buried my face in his pec, and nodded.

Webb dried me off with a big towel, his touch reverent and gentle like I might break. He half carried me to the laundry room and dressed us both in clean underwear and T-shirts. It wasn't until my shirt fell past my hips that I realized Webb had put one of his own shirts on me, but when I saw the look of satisfaction in Webb's eyes, I realized he'd done it on purpose.

A few moments later, we were cuddled together in the swing on the back porch, my legs over Webb's thighs and his arms around me as we swayed gently. Silently.

The sun had passed below the treetops on the far side of the Pond Orchard, and a warm, apple-scented breeze blew through my damp hair. In the pasture, one of the milk cows—probably Stella, the one Gage insisted was an "agitator" who'd eventually "incite a bovine rebellion, you guys, mark my words"—gave a plaintive moo that suggested it was nearly milking time.

A little ways up the road that led to Pond Pond, this autumn's crop of heirloom apple varietals was still green on the vine, and beyond that, my ladies—the little flock of Romeldales I'd originally acquired, plus two generations of their babies—were feasting on summer grass, knowing in the instinctive way that animals always knew that they should make the most of summer's bounty while they could. In just a handful of weeks, the seasons would change, and I'd kiss my husband and stepson goodbye in the mornings before heading to the elementary school to teach a fresh crop of second graders about multiplication tables, and poetry, and the golden rule of friendship.

The life I lived wasn't just different from any life I'd thought I'd have; it was a freaking miracle. So much bigger and sunnier than I could have imagined even five years ago when I was flat broke and living in North Carolina... which just went to show that bad luck didn't last and shockingly good things happened all the damn time.

I just wished I could make Webb see that.

"Can you imagine," I found myself asking, "what would have happened if I hadn't won that contest and come to the Hollow? Or, God, what if we hadn't gotten drunk and blown the bugle down at the Tavern that winter night?"

Webb's arms tightened around me. "I don't even want to think about that. If either of us had done even one thing differently…" His voice trailed off.

I set my hand on his cheek and turned him toward me. "But, Webb, doesn't that mean that sometimes things work out even better than we intend just as often as they go wrong? I mean, neither of us *planned* to find ourselves accidentally married, or to fall in love, or to have this beautiful life. If you'd had a plan at all, it probably involved a woman, and Katey Valcourt at Panini Jack's is probably still low-key hoping you come to your senses."

He huffed out a laugh.

"Before I met you, I'd been knocked around by life a bunch, and so had you. We both had every reason to believe that happily ever afters weren't meant for us. But if we'd kept trying to protect ourselves from getting hurt, we'd have missed out on all of this." I waved a hand to indicate the orchard I loved, the man I hopelessly adored. "Our life happened because we took risks. Because we kept hoping and let our hearts be open to it. Because we worked hard and stuck together."

"You're right. I know you're right." Webb blew out a long, slow breath and threaded our fingers together. "I've been an asshole, haven't I?"

"No, not an asshole, per se, but…"

Green eyes full of regret met mine. "But I let myself get paralyzed by fear, and I pushed you away." He looked out at the pasture. "I'm scared we'll be disappointed again—it seems like all I hear these days are the horror stories—but I tried to keep it to myself. I thought by not talking about my fears, I was being strong for you and not ruining your excitement. I was specifically trying *not* to hurt you. But I did, didn't I?"

He was so serious. So solid and dependable. So very *good*. And so very misguided.

"You pulling away hurts me more than anything, Webb." I shifted to look at him more fully. "Our life is amazing, but it's never going to be perfect. There are going to be bad times. Heartbreaks, like the ones we've had. But I don't need you to be strong and protect me from them. I need you to be beside me, sharing the bad times *and* the good ones." I took a deep breath and admitted, "I thought maybe you regretted trying again."

Webb's eyes widened in horror. "Ah, baby, no. Fuck, no. Never. I… I want this. More than I can even explain. I want to grow our family, and I love those babies so much already. I just… I don't know how to reconcile myself to it, you know? Loving them and feeling so fucking helpless that something could happen to them before they're even here. You'd think I'd be used to that feeling after having Aiden, but this is different. It's like we're an extra step removed, you know? It's hard to believe that it's really happening, that it's really going to be okay."

"I feel the same. But seeing the ultrasound pictures—" I hesitated, half expecting Webb to throw me off his lap and go find a chore that needed done, but his gaze remained steady. "It made me fall in love with them even more. They're *real*, Webb. Little arms and legs and fingers—"

"And noses?" Webb supplied, showing he *had* been listening earlier. He smiled slowly. "I think… No, I *know* I'd like to see that. And then… and then maybe we can start talking about the nursery. We've only got five months to plan, right?"

Unexpected tears made my eyes burn and my vision

waver. "Right! Hardly any time at all. So maybe we should tell everyone that they're coming?"

Webb nodded. "You're right. We should— Wait." He froze for a second, and then he scooped me off his lap, set me on my feet, and grabbed my hand. "I have something to show you. Something you're really going to love. Let's go upstairs right now."

"Is the thing your… bugle?" I demanded. "Because if so, I'm going to need at least ten more minutes to recover first."

Webb threw back his head and laughed, sounding lighter and freer than he had in months. Then he gave me another of those Webb Sunday kisses that made my head spin and my dick perk up more than I'd thought possible.

"Make it five minutes," I said breathlessly, my lips still clinging to his. "Possibly two if you keep kissing me."

He laughed again. "Is this what Knox and Gage meant about getting *very* lucky with the rooster? Because if so, Pecky is definitely double-underline-worthy," he said.

Then he brought me upstairs and proved it.

CHAPTER SIX

WEBB

THE WORST PART about hosting a secret baby-announcement-cookout for the bunch of weirdos who had all, at one time or another, called Sunday farmhouse home wasn't the food prep or the tidying.

It wasn't the chaos or the noise, which were basically family traditions.

It definitely wasn't that my siblings and their partners felt relaxed and comfortable enough to kick off their shoes, fetch their own drinks, and flop on our couch.

It wasn't even that I had to try to be sociable, when what I'd really wanted to do after a day in the orchard was bring my husband upstairs and continue making up for the week of sex I'd denied us.

It was that my uncle didn't trust me to man my own damn grill.

"Back up, firebug," Drew said, hip-checking me out of the way and snatching my tongs from my hand. "You're not burning another batch of drumsticks on my watch."

"That happened one time!" I protested.

"At least twice that I recall." Jack—my now-former best

friend—popped open a beer and took a seat next to Hawk on the porch stairs.

"More like half a dozen," my traitor sister, Emma, said from her perch on the porch railing, daring to sound aggrieved.

"Face it, Webb, you're kind of a repeat offender." Gage looked up from his phone with a pitying glance. "Drew's taking the tongs for your own good."

I narrowed my eyes and crossed my arms over my chest. "You know, that reminds me, Gage, I have the most amazing thing to show you over by the barn. Come see!"

Gage started to rise, but Knox leaned over and put a proprietary hand on his thigh, keeping Gage beside him on the porch swing. "Don't fall for it, baby," Knox said mildly. "The 'amazing' thing Webb wants to show you is the cow pasture. He's going to pretend he can understand what the cows are saying and tell you he's uncovered their plots." Knox paused before adding, "Again."

"Wait, really?" Gage's jaw dropped. "That wasn't funny the first time, Webb. The coming bovine uprising is no laughing matter."

"But hearing Webb teach you how to speak cow was hilarious," Hawk said.

"I think cows speak French anyway," Porter said, apropos of nothing, from his rocking chair by the steps. "At least the evil, plotty ones do."

Gage and I exchanged a confused look. Gage shrugged and made a drinking motion with his hand, but I shook my head. Porter hadn't been drinking, but he *had* been acting weird ever since he and Theo had brought Aiden and Bear home.

"Is there, ah, any particular reason for that, Porter?" Jack wondered.

"Hmm? Oh. No." Porter darted a glance through the

screen door, where his boyfriend was helping Marco and Luke prep appetizers. He rocked his chair harder. "No reason at all."

"Anyone hungry for appetizers?" Luke called. "Marco's outdone himself in here."

"Sick, bruh! I'm *starving*!" Aiden ran in from the yard, where he and Bear were playing fetch, sensitive as usual to any call for food. "Uncle Porter and Uncle Theo only have seedy wheat bread at their house, and that's barely even real bread."

"Didn't stop you from eating half a loaf of it at breakfast, traitor!" Porter called as Aiden ran past.

Chuckling, I clapped a hand on Porter's shoulder as we followed Aiden inside.

While the others helped themselves to Marco's bacon-wrapped dates, hummus with za'atar, and a tray of miniature goat cheese tarts, I caught my husband, wrapped an arm around his waist, and pulled him into the corner.

Luke's smile was extra radiant today. "You ready for this?" he whispered.

To my surprise, I really was… and that was all thanks to Luke. I'd known for years that our relationship was different from any I'd ever had and that with him, a burden shared truly was a burden halved. Somewhere in my blind panic, though, I'd let myself forget that, and I was fucking grateful that my patient, tenacious husband had reminded me.

It took a special person to let you know when you were being an asshole but make you feel loved and understood while doing it.

"We'll make the announcement at dinner," I confirmed. "Five bucks says Drew cries."

Luke laughed. "I don't take sucker bets, baby."

Aiden sat on the kitchen floor with the dog's head in his lap and a plate of food in one hand, recounting every detail of his sleepover to Emma and Knox. "So I was Aragorn, and Uncle Porter was the mountain with the ghosts—"

"*You will not enter here,*" Porter called in a deep voice from the counter where he'd been conscripted into helping Marco whip up a batch of his famous potato salad. "*You are not of the line of Isildur.*"

"—and Uncle Theo was Gandalf… well, until he had to go do an emergency Zoom meeting. And then he put his cape on Bear like this." Aiden waved his free hand around the dog's head in a dramatic reenactment of a cape flourish.

"I think you mean I bestowed my mantle upon Bear, son of Barkmir," Theo said as he sank into a chair at the table with a fresh beer. "For he is wise beyond his kibble and brave beyond his breed."

Aiden chortled. "Yeah, that. And then Uncle Porter made hot fudge, and Uncle Theo eventually got off Zoom after, like, six *hours*—"

"More like one hour, kiddo," Theo protested, laughing.

"More like three." Porter gave the potato salad an exceptionally energetic stir that made Marco *tsk* and push him aside with a sharp "We're not beating eggs here, Porter."

"And then we all turned on the movie and ate Sunday sundaes, and Uncle Theo helped me work on my Aragorn voice." Aiden cleared his throat and sat up straight, one hand resting dramatically on Bear's head like a battle-worn general addressing his troops. In a low, raspy voice, he declared, "*Fight for me, and I will hold your bones sacred!*"

Emma and Knox clapped politely.

"Wow," Luke said, clearly impressed. "Excellent."

Aiden added in his regular voice, "And then Bear sneezed, which kind of ruined the vibe, but it was still awesome, and we stayed up pretty much all night."

"Not quite," Porter and Theo corrected in unison. They shared a look, but Porter quickly turned away to grab something from the fridge.

"See what you're missing, Em?" Theo teased. "Not too late to transfer from UVM to Hannabury and take my Shakespeare seminar."

"Oooh, hard pass," Emma said. "You grade too hard."

"Moi?" Theo pressed a hand to his chest. "Lies and calumny. I'm extremely fair."

She lifted an eyebrow. "Porter had to take your class twice 'cause he failed the first time, and *he's* the love of your life."

"So he says," Porter agreed in a voice so aggressively cheerful that Luke and I exchanged a worried look.

Before I could really think about it, though, Drew and Marco's voices rose from outside.

"I'm just saying you don't need to keep every concert tee you've ever sweated through," Marco snapped. "That's what downsizing's all about."

"But those shirts might be worth something someday!" Drew argued, gesturing wildly with the grill tongs. "I'm going to pass them to my nephews and niece."

"Look out, kids," Marco said dryly. "Twenty years from now, one of you might inherit a size XXL Indigo Girls concert T-shirt Drew bought in Hampton Beach in 1997, complete with marinara dribbles down the front from a mozzarella stick he ate in 2001. Balance your retirement portfolios accordingly."

Everyone laughed, even Drew.

Marco kissed Drew's cheek, soft and sure. It was still strange seeing them open like that after years of keeping their relationship under wraps, but it was good. Really good. As Luke might have said, a reminder that amazing things happened when you kept the faith.

"It's not the shirts that are important," Marco said gently. "The experiences you had, the memories we've made… that's what matters. And I want us to make more memories. Together. That's why we're doing this, remember? So we can travel more."

"I know." Drew gave him an affectionate look, then grunted. "But stop throwing out my stuff before I've had a chance to go through it, okay? It's a *process*."

Marco had the grace to look guilty. "Alright," he agreed. "No more."

"That'll be us someday." Jack leaned back in his chair, slung his arm around Hawk, who was seated beside him, and nodded toward Drew and Marco. "We'll be an old married couple, still passionately in love."

"Yeah." Hawk leaned into Jack and sighed. Then he added, "But you better not get any ideas about downsizing my throw blankets."

"Wouldn't dream of it," Jack assured him, tilting his chair back.

Gage and Knox exchanged a look, and when Knox nodded, Gage grinned. "So, ah… turns out Knox and I will be an old married couple someday, too." He held up his hand, displaying the band on his finger. "I made an honest man of your brother… whatever that expression means."

Jack set his chair down with a thud. "Hell yeah! Congratulations, you two!"

A round of loud back-slapping and congratulatory hugs ensued, deafening even for someone used to Sunday family chaos.

"Hang on. You two have been together forever," Porter teased. "Surely you've already had a wedding—"

Gage punched Porter in the shoulder. "I think I'd remember, jerk."

"Okay, okay!" Laughing, Porter held up his hands. "I must've dreamed it up."

"Yeah?" Knox punched Porter's other shoulder, less gently. "Stop dreaming of my fiancé, Porter."

While everyone was laughing, I nudged Luke and nodded toward the hallway. He tapped Aiden on the shoulder, and the three of us slipped into my home office.

"Bruh, come on, we're missing the fun," Aiden complained, but when Luke grabbed an envelope off my desk, clutched it in his hand, and gave him a nervous smile, he wrinkled his nose. "What's going on?"

"Aiden." Luke licked his lips. "Being your bonus parent is pretty much the best thing that ever happened to me, right up there with marrying your dad. You know that, right?"

"Well, yeah," Aiden said, like it was the most obvious thing in the world.

I tipped my chin to my chest to hide my smile. Luke wasn't just the perfect man for *me*; he was also the perfect stepfather for Aiden. One who never missed an opportunity to show Aiden how important and loved he was. I couldn't *wait* to see him with our daughters.

"So your dad and I decided you might want to, ah… level up." Luke smiled. "From only child to big brother."

For a moment, Aiden's eyes widened, and his mouth formed a perfect, shocked circle. Then he cracked.

"Oh my God, are you *serious?*" he exclaimed, his voice high-pitched with excitement, all traces of preteen cool obliterated. "We're having a baby?"

"Two babies," I corrected as Luke pulled the ultrasound pictures he'd printed out of the envelope. "Twin sisters, dude."

Aiden ran a hand through his hair in a gesture that reminded me of… well, *me*. "This is epic! When are they coming?" he demanded, looking around the room like we might've been hiding actual infants behind my office chair. "What are their names?"

"We've got a few months to prepare and decide that stuff. You're the first person we've told, of course." Luke shrugged fake-casually. "Since they're your family too. Big brother privilege and all."

Aiden stood a little straighter. "Yeah. I mean… obviously. I, ah, don't have to change diapers, do I?"

"Of course not," Luke said at the same moment I said, "Only the really stinky ones."

Aiden grinned wildly.

"We figured you might want to help us tell everyone out there our news during dinner." I nodded toward the chaos in the kitchen. "So we got you this."

Aiden reached into the gift bag I handed him and pulled out a T-shirt. When he read the groan-worthy slogan splashed across the front of it, he rolled his eyes. "You mean *you* got me this, Dad," he countered. "Luke would never."

Luke covered his mouth with his hand, but his eyes danced.

"You're right," I admitted. "It was all me."

In truth, I'd bought the shirt months ago, right after Josie had told us she was pregnant. Because despite the fear that nearly choked me whenever Luke tried to talk about it, those babies had twined themselves around my heart from the first minute. I'd already loved them and wanted them fiercely. And deep down, I hadn't stopped hoping because…

"*Because you're their dad,*" Luke had told me last night with tears in his eyes when I'd pulled the shirt out of the box I'd kept hidden at the top of my closet. Then he'd pushed me onto our bed and kissed me passionately.

Double-underline passionately.

"I'm gonna go put this T-shirt on under my other shirt, and you can give me a signal when you want me to pull it off for the big reveal," Aiden said, catching on immediately. "Don't tell 'em without me, okay?"

"Obviously not," Luke agreed.

Aiden hesitated only a fraction of a second, then threw himself into Luke's arms and gave him a quick, hard hug. "I love you, too, you know," he muttered. He turned to me and repeated the gesture. "Both of you." Then he ran out of the room, clutching his new shirt.

"Wow." Luke blew out a shaky breath. "That was…"

"Amazing? Even better than I'd expected? Yes, to all of it." I pulled him into my arms and buried my face in his neck. "By trying to keep my fear to myself, I almost cost Aiden and everyone the chance to feel this joy."

"But you didn't. Because you're brave. And *good*." Luke wrapped his arms around my neck and lowered his voice to a whisper. "And really, really hot, too. In case I haven't mentioned that today—"

"Yeah?" I nipped at his jaw. "Because I was thinking, after everyone goes home—"

"Hey, Webb? Luke?" Hawk called as he came down the hall. He appeared in the doorway a second later. "Uncle Drew is nearly done at the grill, so—oh my God, *Pecky*?" He goggled at the rooster, which Luke had moved to the table by my office door during our frenzied tidying earlier. "What are you doing here?"

Then his gaze swung to Luke and me, locked together, and he pointed at us accusingly. "I *knew* it was real! You've fallen under the rooster's spell, haven't you? And to think, Jack nearly had me convinced it was just a cookie jar!"

Luke and I exchanged a glance, and I noticed he was fighting not to laugh at Hawk's histrionics.

"No spells, Hawklet," I said mildly. "Just embracing my husband. Fully clothed. In our home. It's a thing we do from time to time."

"Oh, sure, you're fully clothed *now*." Hawk rolled his eyes. "But tell me you weren't both thinking sex thoughts."

I opened my mouth to argue but found that I couldn't. Luke blushed.

Hawk grinned. "Ha! The Cock of Good Fortune is *real*. Wait until I tell Gage."

"It wasn't the rooster—" I began, but when Luke started laughing, I gave up and decided to kiss my husband instead.

By the time we got to the kitchen, everyone had taken their seats at the big farmhouse table, which had been expanded with an extra leaf to accommodate everyone, and Hawk was already in the middle of recounting his story.

"—and Webb was *smiling,* for no reason whatsoever," Hawk said. He thrust a hand in my direction and smiled smugly. "See that big, goofy grin? That's Cock-induced."

"Actually," I stood by my seat with Luke at my side. "For your information, I happen to have a lot to smile about. Like an incredible husband." I lifted Luke's hand to kiss his knuckles. "An amazing son. And a supportive, if somewhat gullible, family. And…" I took a deep breath.

"Now, Dad?" Aiden whispered from down the table.

"I want it noted that I've been willing to believe from the beginning. He was good luck for us." Gage tapped his ring.

Drew brought a large platter of chicken to the table. "What are you talking about? What was good luck?"

"Yeah," Porter demanded. "That's what I want to know."

Luke squeezed my hand and cleared his throat. "Ahem! Speaking of good luck," he began loudly.

"We didn't get engaged because of the rooster, Goodman!" Knox insisted. "I've been planning to ask you to marry me for years, and you know it."

"Sure, but you might've kept right on planning for another four years if the Cock hadn't helped us, ah…" He darted a glance at Aiden, who was practically vibrating with excitement and hardly paying attention. "Initiate the conversation."

"Right?" Hawk grinned dreamily. "It initiated like *four* conversations for me and Jack. That's the most we've had in a while."

"Jesus." Jack ran a hand over his face.

Porter elbowed Knox in the ribs. "Seriously, *what* are you guys talking about?"

"To be clear." Jack addressed himself to the table at large. "There's no such thing as a Cock of Good Fortune, and even if there were, I wouldn't need it in order to… to… *initiate conversations*. Okay? Because Hawk and I converse regularly. All the time. Consistently. It's just been a busy summer—"

I made a retching noise. "Oh, God, don't make me have to bleach my brain." I held up a hand. "If you guys would freaking listen, we're trying to tell you—"

"I'm with Jack," Knox said, ignoring me. "There's no such thing as a Cock of Good Fortune. It can't perform *magic*, for heaven's sake—"

Aiden jumped to his feet, unable to wait any longer. "Dad and Luke are pregnant! With *two* babies!" he announced. Then he pulled up his T-shirt to reveal the T-shirt beneath, which read "BIG BRUH" in large red letters.

For a moment, there was a silence so profound the room rang with it. No one moved. No one spoke. Ten pairs of eyes goggled at Luke and me.

At length, Knox cleared his throat. "Well," he said. "I stand corrected."

Luke laughed out loud. "Aiden means our surrogate is pregnant," he clarified. "Our twin daughters are due in early December."

"Ahhhh! Even *more* luck!" Hawk jumped up and came around the table to hug Luke, then Aiden, and then me. "Have you considered naming them Marianne and Eleanor?" he wondered. He shot Luke a wink. "We'll talk."

Knox stood and slapped me on the back, grinning broadly. "I'm starting their college funds immediately."

"Could someone *please* explain—?" Porter began.

"Merciful. Heavens," Drew whispered. Then he burst into loud, drenching tears. "Did you hear that, Marco? More babies to love!"

"I know, honey." Marco pulled a handkerchief from his pocket, ready as usual to dry Drew's tears, and planted a quick kiss on the side of Drew's head. "It's wonderful."

"You owe me five bucks," I whispered in Luke's ear.

"Ha. I didn't take your bet, Sunday," Luke reminded me,

laughing. "I've been around for a while now, and I know all of you too well."

Later, after we'd finally eaten dinner and then dessert, after Luke had broken out the ultrasound pictures and gotten everyone to agree that yes, one daughter definitely had my nose, after we'd cleaned up and put the leftovers away, Aiden began yawning and slumping in his seat, and the rest of the family got to their feet and began the ridiculously long process of saying goodbye.

Luke and I, along with Emma, Aiden, and Bear, followed them out to the front yard. After a few false starts while Drew ran inside to grab a box of Christmas decorations he'd been storing in the basement, and Gage ran inside to use the bathroom before his arduous, five-minute walk home, and Porter remembered that he'd wanted to take his old hiking backpack from the front hall closet, we waved them off.

When we got inside, Aiden didn't protest going to bed—a sign he and Porter really *had* stayed up most of the night before—Emma left to spend the evening with friends, and I finally got to be alone with the man who'd been filling my life with ordinary miracles for three and a half years.

"Looks like the weather's finally cooling off a bit, huh?" Luke said. He stopped in the living room to plump the pillows and turn off the lamp. "Though I checked my app, and it says we have another five days of—*oh!*"

I grabbed my husband by the waist and crowded him against the wall by the front stairs.

"Luke Sunday, have I told you recently that loving you is the greatest gift of my life?"

Luke blinked. "I… well, not in so many words, but—"

"Our life together is worth every meddling Hollowan trying to commandeer our hand fasting, every icy dunk in the pond—"

"Easy for you to say when I was the one who got dunked," Luke laughed, though his eyes were shiny.

"Every pint of *my* ice cream you stole from me—"

"It was at the grocery store, Webb! By definition, it wasn't—"

"Every scroll-reading we endured, even the one that used the word 'borderethed'—"

Luke laughed harder.

"Because you love me as I am, even when I'm not strong, even when I'm terrified. And you make me feel safe. You make me feel free." I kissed him gently, then pulled back and smiled. "And right now, I'm going to show you exactly how much I appreciate that by taking you upstairs and doing something you really love to do."

"Yeah?" Luke grinned through his tears. "You gonna show me your bugle, Webb Sunday?"

"Who, me? No way. I figured I'd watch you crochet while we ate ice cream and talked about baby names."

Luke made a noise like a pterodactyl and launched himself into my arms, twining his arms around my neck and kissing me until I forgot my own name.

"Why, Luke Sunday!" My dramatic impression of Hawk was a bit breathless since Luke continued peppering my face and neck with kisses. "This is so unexpected! I can't imagine what's gotten into you! You *must* be under the influence of the rooster!"

I pointed at the table by my office door, where Pecky sat.

But to my surprise, Pecky wasn't there.

"Uh, Luke." I pulled away just slightly, though Luke gripped my neck harder and kept kissing me. "Baby, where *is* the rooster?"

"What?" Luke glanced at the table and blinked uncomprehendingly. "Dunno. Someone must've moved it, or maybe Hawk took it home."

I frowned. "Hawk didn't have anything with him when he left. And I swear it was right there when we went outside—"

Luke gripped my face with two surprisingly firm hands

and forced me to look at him. "Webb, do you want to find the Cock of Good Fortune right now? Or can we go upstairs and make another cock really happy?"

Luke's voice suggested there was only one good answer to this question, and as usual, my husband was right.

"Lead the way, baby," I said.

PORTER AND THEO

CHAPTER SEVEN

PORTER

THEY SAY love makes you do crazy things, and I believed that wholeheartedly.

One might say that love (unrecognized, at the time) had led me to recite angry sonnets at my former English professor's cabin on a snowy night. Love had made him give me shelter when he could've left my drunk ass out in the snow. And love had turned our one-night stand into a capital-*R* relationship, despite the potential complications from Theo dating a student.

But standing in a walk-in closet, sweating like a sinner at a revival while trying to hide a possibly magic rooster behind a stack of Theo's old sweaters?

This *might* be a bridge too far down the path to crazy-town for even love to excuse.

"Porter?" Theo's voice called from the living room. "Babe, where'd you go?"

"Coming!" I called. I draped Theo's old cardigan over the chicken… which made it look an awful lot like a cardigan-draped chicken, so I pulled it off again.

Fuck, I was bad at subterfuge.

In general, this was a good thing. I didn't like lying, and I especially didn't like lying to the man I loved. But when Hawk had finally explained to me and Theo what the fuck they'd been talking about at dinner earlier—that he'd found the rooster he'd dubbed the "Cock of Good Fortune" at a rummage sale last weekend, that it was "powerful," and that it had "made me and Jack closer than ever, *if you know what I mean*"—well, I'd been intrigued, even though I knew Theo had probably pulled a muscle restraining his eye roll.

And when it was time to go home, I'd done what any wildly in love, mildly desperate man would do.

I'd smuggled the cock home with me.

Now that I had it, though, I wasn't sure what the fuck I was supposed to do with it. Did it just… sense your need and bestow its favors? Hawk hadn't mentioned any magic words, and there was no handy On switch. I really hoped it wasn't one of those things that needed to be charged under the full moon because I didn't have that kind of—

"Porter?" Theo's voice was closer now. Right outside our bedroom.

I whirled around, leaned fake-casually against the closet doorframe with my arm above my head, and adopted a pose I considered sexy but natural. You know, just enough flex to make the shoulders pop, not enough to actually make them *pop*.

"Porter, seriously, are we playing hide-and—? *Oh.*"

Theo stood in the bedroom door and blinked, taking me in from my decades-old Sunday Orchard T-shirt to my probably equally old athletic shorts and flip-flops. He lifted one dark eyebrow. "Practicing our thirst traps, are we? Is this why you sprinted in from the car and pretended you didn't hear me calling you?"

"Sprint? Pfft. I didn't *sprint*." I straightened, a little annoyed that my beloved was calling me out that way, but also a little proud because I was almost positive my professor had never used "thirst trap" in a sentence before we met, and definitely a little amused because… well, he had a point.

"If I didn't hear you, it's probably that the cabin is so much bigger now than it used to be," I said, not quite able to look him in the eye. "Not like back when we first got together, huh? When we only had one room, we couldn't help seeing each other every minute of every day! I couldn't take a deep breath without bumping into you. Man, those were some good times."

Theo frowned like he was concerned I was having some kind of amnesiac event and… well, he might have a point about that, too. When Theo and I had first gotten together, the cabin hadn't just been cozy but *tiny*, making it hard to have family over or for both of us to work at the same time. No one in their right mind would be nostalgic for those days.

And the truth was, when we'd put on the first addition—our bedroom suite—a few months into our relationship, I'd been so thrilled I'd promised the contractor who'd helped us that we'd name our first daughter after her. Theo had been so starry-eyed over our big bathtub, our walk-in closet, and our room with a door he hadn't even argued, despite us having no plans to have a daughter at all, let alone to name her Jimmi-Lou. It had been that incredible.

But our second addition, last fall, of a home office where Theo could work uninterrupted? That might have *seemed* practical at the time, but in the last couple of weeks, I'd realized it was the worst idea we'd ever had. A soul-crushing nightmare. I mean, not to be dramatic or whatever.

"Porter, baby." Theo walked closer and put his hands on my shoulders, his touch so warm and grounding that despite everything, I wanted to lean into him. "What's wrong?"

"Wrong?" I shook my head. "Why would you think something was wrong? One of my favorite brothers is having a baby—actually, *two* babies—and one of my favorite brothers just got engaged, and one of my favorite brothers is getting married this fall, which means my *other* favorite brother is going to come back from New York and bring his husband, who makes charcuterie! How could I be less than thrilled?"

The words were like a high-pitched avalanche, gathering speed and strength as they spilled out of me.

"And things at Hannabury Hub are great," I went on. "Super great! We got that extra money from the Hannabury Fund, which means we're installing ten new laptops for the after-school program, *and* we're piloting a new mentorship initiative with the high school in the fall. The kids are pumped. *I'm* pumped."

"Porter—"

I sucked in a breath. "And *you*! Things are going amazing at *your* work, too, right? I mean, you haven't talked about your new project very much. Or at all, really. But you've been really busy, and you seem happy? Right? You are happy, aren't you?"

Theo, in his dress shorts and button-down, gave me the sort of look that felt like a hug and an interrogation under Klieg lights all at once. His glasses had slipped down his nose, and when he pushed them up with one finger, it was so freaking cute I felt an irrational spike of fondness.

"I have no idea what's going on with you right now," Theo began conversationally.

"I told you—"

"But," he went on, "if I can read *Beowulf* in the original and figure out what my English 101 students are trying to express, I can figure out what you're not saying, too. I speak fluent Porter. I can *learn to read what silent love hath writ*."

"Sonnet 23," I murmured grudgingly.

Theo smiled, clearly pleased. "Exactly." Theo tapped his lip with one long finger. "So let's piece together what we know, shall we?"

I almost laughed. That response was *so* Theo. And *fuck*, but I loved him for it.

When we'd first gotten together, I knew people questioned whether our relationship would last, and I didn't blame them. On paper, Dr. Theo Hancock, PhD, head of the English Department at Hannabury College, beloved by students and terror of the administration, didn't have much in common with Porter Sunday, orchard kid turned community center director.

But in practice? We worked. We really worked.

We'd always shared passions, like books, and hiking, and home improvement, and we'd expanded each other's horizons over the years, too. Theo genuinely enjoyed hanging out with the kids at the youth center I ran, he fit with my family like he'd always been there, and he'd even admitted—though only once, in a mutter he refused to repeat—that he enjoyed when I dragged him to two-dollar Marvel movie rerun nights at the campus theater.

While I couldn't precisely say that I *loved* Shakespeare, not the way Theo did, I *had* recited a couple of original naughty sonnets for him on our anniversary, *and* I'd won us first prize at the faculty's Halloween family carnival, thanks to the way my legs filled out my hose and doublet, which was sort of close to the same thing.

More than that, though, we complemented each other. Theo's tendency to be overly serious couldn't withstand an impromptu Porter Sunday kitchen striptease. My bad habit of biting off more than I could chew—"Sure I can help you with your grant proposal the same week I present next year's budget to the board while half my staff is out with flu!"— would have really gotten me into trouble if not for Theo's organized brain breaking every task into color-coded action items. And in bed? Explosions. Fireworks. The kind of synchronicity I hadn't known was possible.

Which meant that, all in all, there wasn't a single thing

about my relationship with Theo Hancock that I wanted to change. Nothing about the man that I didn't down-to-my-bones adore.

Theo's phone buzzed. He pulled it out of his pocket, glanced at the screen, and smiled. A small, private kind of smile.

Okay, maybe there *was* one thing I wouldn't mind changing…

"Was that Remy again?" I asked, trying to sound light. "Does he have a new couplet for you to, ah… parse?"

Theo slid the phone away. "Something like that. I have to get back to him later. But first, I'm parsing my boyfriend." He looked me over, studying me like one of the annotated texts on the shelves in his office. "Let's work our way backward from now. You were definitely acting odd at your brother's house earlier—"

I snorted. "Like *that* means anything. I'm always odd. Just ask Knox."

"No," Theo said with a seriousness that surprised me. "You aren't. You're bold, and thoughtful, and competent. You're *joyful*, and you make the people around you, including me, joyful too. But the past little while, it's felt like somebody dimmed your sparkle. You ready to tell me about it?"

Tears, unnecessary and unwelcome, stung the backs of my eyes. When Theo looked at me like that—like he really saw me and took me seriously as a person—it was nearly impossible *not* to want to tell him about it. But the truth was not only low-key humiliating, but it might actually make Theo feel bad. So instead, I did the super-mature thing.

"No, thank you," I said politely. Then, I bolted for the kitchen.

Theo followed me, persistent man that he was, and found me rinsing plates and putting them in the dishwasher.

"I love having Aiden here, but damn we make a mess, huh?" I commented. "Sorry I didn't get to all this earlier."

"Baby, since when do you apologize for making a mess in your own kitchen?"

Since never. But I couldn't help thinking that *Remy* wouldn't leave dishes in the sink overnight. Just like *Remy* wouldn't have stolen his brother's magic ceramic poultry in a fit of panic or required his boyfriend to parse him like he was written in Morse code. But that was because Remy—aka Dr. Remi-Joseph Vessy—was everything I was not.

Remy was urbane and French. He wore scarves unironically. He rolled his *r*'s in a way that made the most basic things—like "ah, you are Theo's Por-tair, non?"—sound sexy and not patronizing. He had *literary* freaking *tattoos* down one forearm. And most annoyingly of all, he'd recently found a rare, annotated quarto of *Love's Labour's Lost*—one of Shakespeare's early comedies—at a small museum in Paris and had come to Vermont to ask his old pal Theo to collaborate on an academic paper about it.

Cue twice-weekly Zoom calls with Remy back in France—private ones, in Theo's home office—and Theo spending his summer break working as hard as he did during the school year.

Cue plans to co-present the paper at some symposium this summer.

Cue my boyfriend absolutely *glowing* ever since.

And cue me, for the first time in my life, feeling acutely, horrifyingly, irrationally jealous… and guilty as fuck about it.

I was not an insecure person by nature. I was comfortable in my own skin, I was confident in my relationship, and I wanted Theo to have as much career success and fulfillment as it was possible for a person to have. I'd joked once, early in our relationship, that I knew Shakespeare was Theo's first love and that if the bard ever got himself reincarnated, I'd generously grant Theo a hall pass.

But when it suddenly felt like that reincarnation had come in the form of a tight-bodied Frenchman whose smirk spoke of inside jokes from when he and Theo had been friends in grad school *and* an obvious interest in doing more than discussing rhyming couplets with my boyfriend? Well, I'd freaked out a little.

And by a little, I meant a lot.

I'd been trying for weeks to get a handle on it. I'd told myself firmly that I had no right to feel this way since I knew Theo loved me. I'd scolded myself that it was mean and unfair of me to feel this way since I knew Theo would never cheat on me physically or emotionally. I'd berated myself for being immature as fuck and not living up to my own expectations. And I could not tell Theo about any of it because that would make it *his* problem when I knew it was mine and only mine.

Like, how lowering would it be if he felt like he needed to reassure me when he hadn't done anything to make me doubt?

"Now that I think about it," Theo said, leaning back against the counter by the sink, still studying me, "you've been acting strangely for a few weeks. I offered to go see *Thor: Ragnarok* at the revival theater, and *you* suggested we go to a student production of *Much Ado About Nothing*. Which you hate."

"I don't hate the whole play," I muttered. "I just hate that Hero pays the price for Claudio's pride and jealousy, and then she forgives him in the end, and we're all supposed to clap."

Theo shrugged. "Well, *reason and love keep little company together*, right?"

I squinted at him, trying to remember if I'd heard that quote before, then shook my head. "I don't know that one."

"*As You Like It*." Theo's gaze grew abstracted, and he slipped into his deep, resonant professor voice, seemingly on instinct.

It was really fucking adorable. And hot. Hot-dorable.

"Shakespeare's saying that emotions aren't always rational," he said. "They can't exist within the framework of reason. Now, we might take this as a kind of warning that our unreasonable emotions can steer us wrong—like with Claudio. But I like to think it's an acknowledgment of our contrary human nature. And whether Shakespeare would agree or not, I think it's kind of a gift. Imagine never being able to do something as wholly irrational and unreasonable as falling for the hot guy screaming angry sonnets at your house in the dead of night." He stuck his hands in his pockets, and one side of his mouth tipped up in an affectionate grin. "Who'd want to live in that kind of world?"

Throat tight, I shut off the faucet, then turned and twined my damp hands around Theo's neck. "I love you, Theo Hancock," I whispered, staring into those pretty eyes I loved. "You're the most wonderful, unreasonable thing that ever happened to me."

Theo ran his hand through my hair and then cupped the side of my neck. His eyes sparkled. "As the bard himself might have said… 'Same, baby, same.'"

I laughed out loud. And then I pulled him closer and kissed him slow and deep, trying to pour every unspoken thing into it. His lips were warm and firm as they moved under mine, and I pressed in closer, curling my fingers into the hair at the back of his neck. When his strong hands slid up the back of my shirt and he made a low hum like he was already sinking into it, the sound vibrated right down my spine, and I could have cried at the relief of it.

Kissing him was always a little overwhelming, not because he took over—he didn't, usually—but because he paid attention, and being the focus of Theo Hancock's attention was a heady thing. I never felt more right, more confident, more wholly *me* than when I was in Theo's arms.

My heart thumped crazily, like it wanted to leap directly

from my chest to Theo's. My whole body felt keyed up; every millimeter of skin was tuned to Theo's wavelength and hungry for contact, for friction, for the dizzy, helpless, perfect closeness I only ever got with him.

His hand cupped my jaw, holding me still. "You're trying to distract me, Mr. Sunday," he said in an evil Bond-villain voice. "It won't work."

Laughing unsteadily, I pulled him off the counter and manhandled him—backward—through the living room.

"Oh, it will," I murmured against his lips. "It definitely will."

That earned me a grin that was a little crooked, a little wild. "Cocky little shit," he said affectionately.

"*Your* cocky little shit," I reminded him, and his grin got wilder.

"All fucking mine," he agreed with a growl in his voice. He turned us and backed me into the wall by the bedroom door. "*That* was never in doubt." He slid his hands under my shirt again, his palms gliding over my bare skin with uncompromising ownership, pulling the thin material up and over my head.

"Theo," I whispered. "I need—"

"I know what you need." He stepped closer, forcing his muscled thigh between mine. I was still reeling at the welcome intrusion when he grasped both of my wrists in one hand and trapped them against the wall over my head in a pose reminiscent of the one I'd tried earlier. "This is what you've been practicing for, isn't it?"

"Fuck." I laughed breathlessly. It was crazy that even after all this time, he could still make my blood fizz and pound.

"Mine." He dragged his free hand down my abs, snagging at my waistband. Then he moved lower, fondling my already half-hard dick, tracing the shape of it through the silky mesh. "Mine."

My eyes burned again, so I shut them. With a shaky breath, I nodded.

"Mine," he whispered against my lips before kissing me gently. Then he pulled back, waited for my eyes to open and meet his, and set his hand directly over my heart. "Mine," he said once more.

I wasn't sure whether I wanted to tackle-kiss him or burst into tears, but I didn't get a chance to do either because Theo was already moving. With a final kiss to my jaw, he guided me backward into our bedroom and then further, until my knees hit the bed. With a firm push, he sent me down onto the mattress, and I barely had time to gasp before he was straddling me, flipping me, and easing my shorts down my thighs with reverent hands.

He knelt between my legs, kissed my hip bone, and dragged me up to my knees with my legs spread wide, my chest and stomach against the mattress. Then he kissed me again, just below the curve of my ass. His hands slid away from my hips and—

Fuck.

Theo gripped my ass in both hands with strong, sure fingers, spread me open, and licked a slow, deliberate stripe over my hole. "Mine," he whispered against my damp skin.

"Theo." I clutched our comforter in both hands and arched involuntarily, caught between squirming away from the overwhelming sensation and pressing back to beg for more. The movement made my dick rub against the bed, and pleasure cracked through me like the lash of a whip.

Theo's tongue circled and pressed, hot and wet and relentless. As he worked me, he made these little hums and groans, encouraging me to rock against the bed and ratchet my own pleasure even higher. My toes curled, my thighs shook, and my breath was reduced to shallow pants in time with my rocking.

Theo never rushed when it counted, and this was no

exception. He worshipped me with a kind of thoroughness that made my bones liquefy, alternately using his tongue to lap at my rim, to fuck my hole, and to murmur obscene things about how good I tasted, how gorgeous I was, how much he wanted me.

I was molten under his mouth, hard and leaking, when I finally wailed, "Fuck me, Theo, *please*."

But when Theo pulled back, I groaned at the loss.

"Roll over, baby," he ordered. "I want you to look at my eyes."

I obeyed on trembling limbs and found Theo's face flushed, his lips wet, his green eyes dark with love and hunger. He climbed up my body and kissed me, fierce and messy. Then he grabbed lube from the nightstand drawer, slicked himself, and guided his cock inside me slowly, his gaze never leaving mine.

My mouth opened on a silent cry as he filled me inch by inch.

He wrapped his lube-slicked fingers around my cock. "This is mine," he said, giving me a single firm stroke.

Then he braced himself over me on one forearm and moved his other hand to swipe a tear from my cheek that I didn't remember shedding. "And this is mine, too," he said fiercely. "Every part of you. Always. Understand?"

I didn't. Not really. My mind had been hollowed out with need and want, and a single thought echoed through it over and over with each beat of my heart. *Theo, Theo, Theo.*

"I love you, Porter," Theo said as he began to move. "I love you endlessly. Every single part of you. And I will never stop."

More tears—where were they coming from?—filled my vision, so I clasped his jaw with both hands and held on as he began to fuck me in deep, hard strokes. Every movement was a possession, a claiming, a vow he was carving into my skin.

It wasn't just the best sex we'd ever had; it was a reckoning. A homecoming. A reminder of every moment over the past three years that had brought us to this place.

It *was* unreasonable to love someone so much, just like Theo had said. Irrational to give another person so much of yourself and trust them to carry it carefully.

But loving Theo was also the safest, sanest thing I'd ever done.

When I came, it felt like falling and flying at once, my whole body drawn tight-tight-tight, then undone in a rush. Theo followed with a shudder, spilling hot inside me while crying my name in a voice full of wonder, like he couldn't believe I was real.

When Theo finally pulled out of me and collapsed at my side on his back, sweat-damp and breathless, neither of us spoke for a long moment. But that was okay because being fucked that way… well, it pretty much said everything, didn't it? Words were extraneous.

Theo turned his head to look at me.

"I love you, Porter Sunday," he said. "In case that wasn't clear."

I laughed—well, wheezed—helplessly, and my heart squeezed. Okay, maybe *not* so extraneous.

"I love you, too," I said. "So much. And I love *us*. I believe in us. Thank you for reminding me how much."

Theo frowned. "Had you forgotten?"

"No. Not really. I…" I hesitated.

He rolled toward me and leaned up on one elbow. "Look, I don't want to pressure you to talk if you're not ready. But I want you to remember there's *nothing* you can't tell me."

I huffed. "Like those 'we listen and we don't judge' TikToks?"

"Yes, exactly. If you're unhappy in this house, or if seeing your brothers get engaged has made you want to do that sooner than we planned, or if you changed your mind and want to, ah, have a… a child," he said, with only a slight quaver in his voice. "I'm not saying I'm ready to do those things immediately, or maybe at all, but we could certainly have a conversation—"

"Not at all?" I blinked guilelessly. "But, honey… what about Jimmi-Lou?"

Theo's eyes widened for a single instant before he realized I was teasing. "Cocky. Little. *Shit*," he said, punctuating each word with a poke to my ribs. "I'm over here baring my heart, telling you that if you want to confess to a fucking murder, I'll help you move the body. And meanwhile, *you*—"

I grabbed his hand in both of mine and kissed it, smiling so wide I felt like my face might crack in two. "I do not want a baby. Quarterly sleepovers with Aiden—and I guess the twins, eventually—is plenty. I do want to get married, probably, but not right now. I want to stay in this house until we're old and gray. And I don't have any bodies to bury. I haven't even angry-sonneted anyone in years."

"You'd better not have," Theo muttered darkly.

I laughed again, burying my face in his neck.

"So, then…?"

At this point, it would have been more ridiculous not to confess, right? I sighed and rolled onto my back, throwing my forearm over my eyes. Theo rolled, too, following me.

"It's silly. And petty. And mean," I began.

"Porter," Theo said in a hushed voice.

"No, seriously. It is. And it's embarrassing. Mortifying, really—"

"Porter," he said again, louder now.

"And I want you to know, it's not an is*sue*, it's an ish-*me*—"

"Porter!" Theo insisted, confused and possibly a bit panicked.

I pulled my arm down. "What? It *is*. And I'd like to point out that I'm only confessing *because* I love and trust you, okay—?"

"Porter." Theo grabbed my chin gently and turned my head so that I faced our walk-in closet. "Why is your brother's sex rooster looking at my dick?"

Sure enough, when I followed his gaze to the closet shelf, there sat Pecky, perched at a crooked angle amongst Theo's sweaters. And he really did seem to be staring at us. *Intently*.

"Fuck," I groaned. "Okay, I can explain."

CHAPTER EIGHT

THEO

PORTER JUMPED OUT OF BED, his hair still mussed and damp from our lovemaking. "Okay, first of all, I'd like to remind you that you said you'd listen and not judge."

I bit the inside of my cheek to restrain my laughter—a reaction I wouldn't have thought possible just a few hours ago.

All evening at Webb's, I'd been watching Porter get more brittle and distant, like glass cooling too quickly. I wasn't entirely oblivious—certainly not where the love of my life was concerned—and I'd seen the signs building for days, but at first, I'd explained them away. Aiden was a freaking delight, but having a kid in the house was always chaotic. And God knew the oppressive summer heat could throw anyone off.

When I'd really stopped to think about it during our mostly silent drive home, though, I'd realized it had been going on longer than I'd allowed myself to acknowledge. A couple of weeks at least.

Guilt had hit me like a physical weight in my chest. I'd been so consumed with this Shakespeare project, so buried in research and correspondence, I hadn't noticed that Porter was struggling. Worse, he clearly hadn't felt like he could come to me about whatever it was.

My mind had quickly spiraled through some worst-case scenarios. Was Porter having second thoughts about us? Was he tired of my academic obsessions?

The thought that Porter might be unhappy had been absolutely terrifying—the kind of terror that made my blood cold despite the heat—and I'd made love to him with a desperate intensity.

But seeing him now, pacing the floor beside our bed unselfconsciously naked, his hair sticking up at impossible angles, while that absurd rooster cookie jar from Webb's house watched from the closet like a poultry voyeur... I somehow felt more settled than I had in days.

Whatever Porter was about to confess couldn't be so terrible, not when we were here together like this. We could handle anything as long as we faced it together.

"I pinky promise," I said. I grabbed a towel from the nightstand to clean myself and sat back against the pillows to watch Porter pace. Though I was genuinely concerned—and genuinely spent—I couldn't help appreciating how the lamplight gilded the lean lines of Porter's muscles.

He ran a hand through his hair, making it even more disheveled. "Okay, so... you heard Hawk's explanation about the rooster earlier?"

"That Sir Pecksworth called to him from amongst the other crockery on the Dishes and Doo-Dads table like it knew him of old? That it practically begged Hawk— mentally, subliminally, *magically*—to take it home and then proceeded to make Hawk's fiancé fuck him all over their house, an activity they've never, ever engaged in before?"

Porter's cheeks flushed pink, and he stopped pacing long enough to cross his arms defensively over his chest. "It wasn't just Jack and Hawk! Something similar happened with Gage and Knox, and then Luke and Webb, too, when they were given the rooster, so—"

"Baby," I interrupted gently, sitting up straighter. "Gage and Knox have been thinking about getting married for years, just like we have. Luke and Webb's surrogate has been pregnant for months. Having been around your brothers—especially after the time we nearly caught Gage and Knox in the orchard—I don't think them having a lot of sex can be solely attributed to Pecky the Magic Rooster."

"The Cock of Good Fortune," he corrected sharply, his jaw tightening. "And just to say... I'm pretty sure you're judging right now."

"But I'm not judging you," I pointed out. "I'm judging people who believe the rooster is—" I stopped mid-sentence as the penny dropped. "Porter, why did you bring the sex rooster home? Do you... I mean... If you're not satisfied with what we..."

"What?" Porter paused in his pacing and wrinkled his nose. "Oh." He waved a hand in angry dismissal as he resumed. "Fuck, no. Our sex life is so good I sometimes have to remind myself why we both need to work full-time jobs. It wasn't about that."

Relief flooded through me. "Right. No. Good. So then what...?"

"The rooster's lucky," he blurted, the words tumbling out in a rush. "Or I hoped he might be. And I needed some luck because... Ugh." He took a deep breath. "I've been jealous, Theo. Weirdly jealous. Stupidly jealous. And I didn't want to tell you because I know how silly it is. That thing Shakespeare said about *reason and love*? He wrote it about me."

I sat up quickly and grabbed Porter's hand, stopping his frantic pacing. "Hold up. Jealous of what? Of who?"

Porter looked at me like the answer should be obvious. "Of Remy. Obvs."

"Remy," I repeated slowly, trying to process this information. "Remy?" My mind conjured up an image of my research partner—good-looking, if you squinted, but mostly hot air and scarves. Lots of scarves. "God, why?"

"Why not?" Porter began ticking things off on his fingers, his voice getting higher with each point. "You're both all in on this exciting project, he knows as much about Shakespearean sonnets as you do, he's got tattoos, he's got that hot accent. And…"

His hands clenched into fists, and he looked off into the corner of the room.

"Remember when you introduced me to him at that reception when he was visiting? He called me 'Theo's Porter' and asked if I was a Shakespeare scholar." Porter rolled his eyes. "And I said, 'Nah, I just sleep with one.' And he said, 'Ah, well, we cannot all be blessed with scholarly minds, can we, Theo?' And you smiled." Porter's voice cracked slightly on the last word, accusation bleeding through the hurt. "You smiled this… this warm, secret smile."

"Oh," I said softly, thinking back to that night but remembering it entirely differently. "I see."

"Look, I know how I sound. I can hear myself." Porter's voice was miserable now, all the fight going out of him, and it made my heart squeeze. "*Unreasonable*, but in a Claudio way. Like the kind of dimwitted child Remy probably thinks I am." He scrubbed a hand over his face. "But no matter how I try to talk myself out of feeling this way, I… I can't. I know you love me, Theo. I know that. But I just… I wonder if there's some part of you that… wishes I was more like him or something. I don't know."

I sucked in a breath through my nose. "Porter, come sit here." I patted the bed beside me.

"Oh, no, thank you. I just *knew* you were going to do this. Be all kind and sympathetic." He glared at me briefly. "Don't make me feel better, or it'll make me feel worse."

I had to fight back another smile. "Please?"

With a sigh, Porter perched on the edge of the bed, his body still tense with anxiety. I began rubbing slow circles on his back, feeling the tight knots of stress in his shoulders gradually start to loosen under my touch.

"So, a couple things," I said at length. "First, this isn't all on you. I've been really consumed with this project. I don't think I realized just how consumed until I started thinking back on it tonight—"

"And that's okay!" Porter interrupted. "That's what I'm trying to say. I'm not a child; I'm a whole-ass adult. And I know Shakespeare's your first love. I know how much your career means to you—"

"Hush." I pressed a finger gently to his lips, feeling their warmth. "Now it's your turn to listen and not judge, okay?"

I waited for his grudging nod before I took my hand away from his mouth and threaded my fingers with his. "Shake-speare's not my first love, Porter. You are."

His eyes went wide, and I could see him trying to process my words. I leaned back against the pillows and pulled him with me, settling him against my chest where I could feel his heartbeat.

"I do love my work. Of course I do," I went on. "For a long time, it was the most important thing in my life. Some might say the *only* thing in my life, after my grandfather died." I gave him a rueful smile. "But that's not true anymore and hasn't been for a long time. *You're* my future, Porter. *You* have my heart. To an *unreasonable* degree."

"But—"

"I'm not done. Do you want to know a secret about Remy? He doesn't know as much about Shakespeare as he likes to pretend he does."

"Reeeeally?" Porter's voice perked up with interest, and I felt some of the tension leave his body.

"Oh yeah." I grinned. "He's ninety-nine percent accent and tattoos. Always has been. I'm only working with him because the project is fascinating. And part of the reason I'm spending so much time on it is because *I'm* doing a lot of the work." I put on an exaggerated French accent and waved my hand dramatically. "'Theo, I am so ov-air-come by ze beauty of zis metaphor zat I cannot write ze analysis as I promised!'"

Porter burst out laughing, the sound bright and genuine, and I felt something tight in my chest finally release.

"You know, I remember introducing you to him at that reception." My arms tightened around him. "I remember exactly what you said—and it was perfect, by the way. Quick and charming, completely you. I even remember smiling. But, baby, that smile had nothing to do with him and everything to do with you. With how lucky I felt to have you beside me, how proud I was that you're mine."

I cupped his face in my hands, stroking my thumbs across his cheekbones, needing him to hear me and believe me. "I know plenty of people who share my passion for Shakespeare. I love that you have your own interests, that your brain works differently than mine, that you think fast and feel deeply, that you have a brilliant, irreverent sense of humor, but you never put people down to make yourself feel good. There is no one on Earth—living or dead, even William Shakespeare himself—I'd rather spend my life with. You've been it for me since that first angry sonnet."

Porter buried his face in my neck, his breath warm against my skin as he whispered, "You know it's the same for me. It's just you, Theo."

He leaned over me further, trailing his fingers down my ribs in a touch that was reverent and wondering. The anxiety that had been pouring off him all evening—and longer—was finally gone, replaced by something tender and hungry.

This time, there was no desperation, no urgency in our connection, just desire. Just love. Just our bodies pressed together, the drag of skin on skin, the press of thighs, the slide of our sweaty chests as we rocked against each other. Porter's mouth found mine, and our kiss spun out until we were simply breathing together.

There was nothing better than making love to Porter. I loved the heat and weight of him on top of me, the feel of his hard cock nudging mine, the way he gasped into my mouth when I rolled my hips just right. His hands framed my face, and his eyes locked to mine, pupils blown wide with arousal and emotion like nothing outside of this bed existed.

I wrapped my hand around both of our cocks, feeling the slick heat of them together as I worked us both. Porter's breathing grew ragged, needy little sounds escaping him with each movement, and my own control started to fray at the edges.

"Theo," Porter groaned as I felt his body tense above me.

We came nearly in unison, shuddering and breathless for the second time that night. He collapsed onto me, and I held him close, my heart thudding so hard I was sure he could feel it against his chest. I *hoped* he could.

"I really wish I'd explained all this earlier," Porter murmured against my shoulder after we'd caught our breath. "I was trying not to burden you with my immature shit—"

"Your emotions aren't a burden, Porter. I want to know how you're feeling, always, because you're mine. *All* of you. Every bit. Even the *unreasonable* stuff." I smiled and pressed a kiss to the top of his head. "You're my soul's other half. My heart's delight. My joy by day, my peace in the night."

Porter frowned thoughtfully, then shook his head. "I don't know that one."

"Because I just came up with it." I smiled smugly. "You're not the only sonnet writer in this family, Porter. You need to share the crown."

Porter grinned, his whole face lighting up with delight. "You make me so happy, Theo Hancock. I love you."

"But can we be *sure*?" I teased, trailing my fingers down

his spine. "Maybe you only *think* you love me. Maybe Pecky's forcing you to say that."

Porter rolled his eyes. "Alright, alright. I might deserve that. Stealing the cock was not my finest hour."

"You stole him?" I demanded, sitting up straighter.

He shrugged. "More like... borrowed. I'll bring him back tomorrow."

I mock gasped. "Grand Theft Poultry, Porter?"

"Hey! You were okay with *murder* a minute ago!"

We both burst out laughing. And as I looked toward the closet where that smug little rooster still sat, watching us with its painted eyes, I felt a kind of joy bubble up inside me that I'd never known before the night Porter Sunday had first shown up at my door.

The rooster might not be magic, but the man in my arms and the love we'd found sure as fuck were.

And I was going to hold on to them forever.

MARCO AND DREW

CHAPTER NINE

MARCO

"Okay, how about this one?" The kitchen chair creaked as I lifted a T-shirt out of the purple storage tote on the floor and held it up for Drew's inspection. "Keep, Toss, or Donate?"

Late-morning sunlight streamed through the kitchen window of the Sunday farmhouse—now Luke and Webb's place—spotlighting all the dust motes Drew and I had stirred up and making the room incredibly hot... at least by most folks' standards.

Drew, who sat cross-legged on the floor in his gauzy "new" caftan printed with pictures of the Golden Girls—one he'd picked up for "a song" at last weekend's charity rummage sale since it "was *just like* one he had at home"— seemed not to feel the heat. He tipped down his red-framed reading glasses and pursed his lips in thought, like whole civilizations might rise or fall based on his choice.

I stifled a sigh. Sorting through decades of assorted clutter was not *my* favorite way to spend a sunny summer day. Not when I could be gardening, or up at the lake with Aiden and Luke, or visiting my granddaughter, or even in bed at home with the air conditioner jacked down so low I'd need to pull out the duvet. But this task was important.

When Drew had finally moved in with me two years ago, he'd left a few things behind in the farmhouse basement so he could take his time sorting through them. I think we'd both underestimated just how long we'd put off the project, though, *and* how long it would take once we finally got started.

Lord knew I'd underestimated what "a few things" meant.

Still, I was determined not to get impatient. Not today. I'd learned my lesson the last time I'd lost my patience and had made a careless mistake as a result. A mistake that was very obviously coming back to bite me in the ass.

If I'd learned one thing in the seventeen years Drew Sunday had been my partner, my lover, and my best friend, it was that there were consequences when the man felt rushed or bossed around.

"Hmmm." Drew leaned toward me and ran a hand over the front of the T-shirt, fingering a spot that was nearly worn through and another where mutant-green speckles dotted the hem. I knew for a fact this shirt was two sizes smaller than anything Drew currently wore. He smiled. "Keep."

I squeezed my eyes shut and blew out a breath. "Drew. Baby. We've been at this an hour already, and we have twenty more storage totes to go through." I pointed at the multicolored containers stacked along the kitchen wall. "You can't keep everything, honey. That's not what downsizing *means*."

"But Marco, that's the shirt I wore when I helped Emma dye her hair green to protest climate change back when she was thirteen, remember? I was so proud my girl was such a justice fighter. I can't just throw it away."

"But—"

"Can't." He lifted his chin in challenge. "Can. Not." He grabbed the shirt from my hand and deposited it in the Keep box, alongside a mix tape labeled "LILITH FAIR ROAD TRIP TUNES 1995!", a construction paper snowman with googly eyes, a cucumber-shaped sugar bowl emblazoned with the words "I GOT PICKLED IN WINSOME," and a rusted aluminum pan.

"This is the twentieth item in a row you're keeping," I pointed out. "Compared to…" I glanced into the Donate and Toss bins and pretended to count on my fingers. "Zero items you've gotten rid of."

"And what would you have me do?" Drew demanded, all dramatic outrage. "Toss the snowman Porter decorated with a pound of glitter because he knew his Uncle Drew would love it? Toss the sugar bowl you and I bought at that adorable little store in Winsome while we were on our first date? Toss the only pan big enough to hold the cheesy broccoli casserole I make our family every Thanksgiving?" He sniffed. "You *love* that casserole, Marco."

Drew's green eyes—eyes that were the last thing I'd seen before falling asleep, five thousand nights running—glittered fiercely, his face flushed pink beneath hair that was a good bit thinner than it used to be, and when he folded his arms over his chest, the caftan pulled against his belly.

He remained the most beautiful man, inside and out, that I'd ever laid eyes on.

I nudged aside the box at my feet and leaned forward to tug on Drew's hands. After a brief show of reluctance, he unclenched his arms and let me twine our fingers together.

"Drew, we said we wanted to spend the next couple of years traveling," I reminded him gently. "To do that, we need to sell off my house and buy a smaller place and a travel trailer. That's still what you want, right?"

His posture relaxed. "Yes."

I nodded. "And you don't want to keep your things in the basement here anymore? Because Webb said—"

"No." Drew shook his head. "He and Luke deserve to have their space."

I nodded again, unsurprised. We'd gone over this repeatedly in the past few weeks. "Then I don't see a way to accomplish those things without giving up some of this ju—" I winced. "Some of these *items*."

The narrow look my lover sent me suggested that he'd heard the word I hadn't said. "I know you don't understand this, but my stuff isn't *junk*, Marco. These are memories. *My* precious memories. My whole life, in boxes and bins. They're who I *am*."

I opened my mouth, probably to put my foot in it, but I was saved by the click of the front door opening, followed by the sound of two men cackling as though they were trying to be quiet and failing.

"Shhhh," Porter's voice said, though he was laughing so hard it came out in staccato bursts. "I thought I was bad at subterfuge, but you're way worse, Professor."

Drew's gaze met mine, and I rolled my eyes. Drew grinned.

"Hey! Unlike some, I never aspired to a life of crime," Theo complained. "Now, hurry up and put the cock back in the kitchen before your brother and Luke get home and realize you stole it."

"*Borrowed* it," Porter corrected. "And now we're returning it."

"*We*? Oh, no. I'm here as your lookout, that's all."

"But baby, we're a team—"

"Not if you're going down for Grand Theft Poultry, Sunday. This pretty face wasn't meant for prison."

Porter snorted. "But if I get locked up, you'll wait for me, right, bab—*oh*." Porter appeared in the kitchen doorway, spotted Drew and me, and stopped dead.

Theo, a pace behind, bumped into him. "*I'm* bad at subterfuge? You can't just—? *Oh*." Theo looked from me to Drew to something tucked under Porter's arm. "Drew! Marco! Nice day, isn't it?"

"Theo," I said mildly. "Porter."

Drew remained silent, folded his arms over his chest, and

looked at Porter, just as he had when Porter was a mischievous child.

"Gosh!" Porter smiled winningly. "*Wow*. This is… this is so great, seeing you both again. So soon. Here in Webb's house. Where we didn't expect to find you. We, ah…" He looked at Theo helplessly.

"We were on our way to the pond to meet Webb and Luke and Aiden," Theo volunteered gamely. He gestured at his swim trunks and flip-flops. "But we stopped here to, um…" He nudged Porter's hip.

"To drop something off," Porter blurted. He set the thing he'd been carrying on the sideboard. "Anyway—"

"Porter Sunday," Drew began.

If I knew Drew—and I did—he'd been intending to tease Porter a little longer, just to see him squirm. But when Porter backed up a pace and Drew saw what he'd been carrying, his jaw and his eyes widened.

So did mine, for an entirely different reason. *Fuck.*

"It's a rooster cookie jar," Porter said unnecessarily. "Hawk bought it."

"Well, I'll be darned." Drew's eyes lit with delight. "I have one just like that. Somewhere." He gestured vaguely at the stacked-up storage totes.

"Similar, maybe," I agreed, a bead of sweat running down the back of my neck that had nothing to do with the warmth in the kitchen. "Sort of. Not really."

"No, it is," Drew insisted. With a hand from Porter, he hauled himself to his feet and went to inspect the rooster. "The resemblance is uncanny!"

"Well, lots of people have things that look alike," I said. "They just buy them at the same places."

Drew turned with the rooster in his hands and gave me a look of rebuke. "Not possible with my rooster. It's one of a kind! I got it at an artists' fair over in Burlington," he explained to Porter and Theo. "It was a summer day as hot as this one, and I was strolling up the aisles looking for some hand-dyed fabric to make harem pants—you remember my harem pants era?"

Porter smiled. "I think everyone in the Hollow remembers that era."

"It hadn't even occurred to me to look at ceramics that day, but suddenly, there was this beauty just gleaming in the sunlight, like the Universe was saying *This! This is what you didn't know you needed, Drew.* So of course, I rushed over to the table... but by the time I got there, someone else was reaching for it."

Theo chuckled. "Ooof. Did you two have words?"

"You better believe it. I told the guy I'd wrestle him for it, and I meant it." Drew clutched the rooster to his chest with one hand and flicked the skirt of his caftan sassily with the other. "I won."

"Hell yeah." Porter held up his hand for a high-five. "You scared him off, and you got the cock."

Drew's mouth twisted up in a tip-tilted smile as he slapped Porter's hand. "I certainly did."

I rolled my eyes.

"And on that note," Theo said dryly, "Porter, the pond?"

"Lead on. We'll see you guys later." Porter grabbed Theo's wrist and stepped in front of him. "On second thought, let *me* lead. Kinda liked it when you ran into me on the way in."

There was the brief sound of a scuffle, followed by Porter's yelp and Theo's laughter, and then the door closed behind them.

Drew chuckled to himself, then turned his attention back to the rooster... exactly where I *didn't* want it. If he looked hard enough at that thing, he was going to realize that *this* rooster had a distinctive chip in its wing precisely where Drew had knocked *his* rooster against the sink one day while cleaning it... and then I was going to be in serious trouble.

"You know, I don't think it's fair to imply that you won a

wrestling match to get the rooster," I said, casually walking over to him. I took the rooster from his hands just as casually and set it on the sideboard. "I *let* you have it. It was a chivalrous gesture."

As I'd known he would, Drew narrowed his eyes and set his hands on his hips. "Chivalry? Is that what we're calling it? I call it blatant flirtation, Marco Vanzetti. You wanted my cock… and I don't just mean the rooster."

I laughed genuinely. "Hardly. I didn't know how to flirt with a hot guy then. I'd barely admitted to myself that I was attracted to men at all. But then suddenly, there was *this* beauty—" I gripped his chin with one hand as I repeated his words from earlier. "Gleaming in the sunlight like the Universe was saying *This! This is what you didn't know you needed, Marco*." I winked. "And I had to have him."

Drew snorted, waving my words away, but his face softened, like he was remembering that day, too. The warmth of the sun and the buzzing of the crowds and how it had all faded to a blurry, gray background noise the minute his hand touched mine.

Drew Sunday was like a prism, crystal-bright and multifaceted, making me see rainbows where none had been before. I'd had a life before him, sure—a failed marriage, a grown daughter, a stable job—but I hadn't known how to *live*.

I looped my arms around his waist and pulled him in for a kiss. "I still feel that way, you know," I said. "Meeting you changed my life."

Drew's eyes met mine, and he blushed just a little, even after all these years. "I admit, it impressed the hell out of me that you managed to track me down after that."

"When all I knew was that you were wearing a shirt that said ORCHARD STAFF, with Drew embroidered on the pocket?" I shook my head. "I think I spent the whole next week making phone calls at my desk when I was supposed to be handling insurance claims. I didn't realize just how many orchards there were in Vermont."

He laughed. "And I like to imagine you calling all of them and choking out, 'Excuse me, ma'am, I'm looking for a man named Drew who took my cock...'"

"Hush." I slapped his ass lightly. "I'm spouting sentimental shit here."

"Yes, you are." Drew frowned suspiciously. "And that's very unlike you."

"Hey! I can be sentimental."

"You can," he agreed, still frowning. "But usually much more subtly and rarely out loud. What gives?"

I chuckled uncomfortably, while the rooster on the sideboard pulsed behind us like a telltale heart, and tried to sidestep. "Do you remember our first date?"

Drew's expression cleared. "When we decided to meet for coffee partway between your place and mine and wound up in that weird little town with the store that was all about pickles? Of course. It was amazing."

Personally, I didn't think anyone who was from the Hollow had standing to call another town weird, but I didn't argue.

"I fell in love with you that day," I told him, though he already knew it. "Didn't matter that I'd never been with a man before, or that you lived nearly three hours away in cow country, or that I had a bad track record with relationships." Hadn't mattered, either, when Drew told me he wouldn't leave the niece and nephews he'd agreed to help raise. "I was all in. I'd recognized what I couldn't live without, and then it was just a matter of doing whatever it took to win your heart and keep it."

"Winning my heart was easy, handsome charmer that you are." Drew touched my cheek gently. "Keeping it, though..." He rolled his eyes.

I smiled ruefully. "I hadn't been anyone's partner in years. I was a bit bossy back then, I know—"

"A bit?" Drew hooted. "Back then?"

I'd swear I could feel that damn rooster's eyes on me. "Possibly a little now, too," I admitted, rubbing at the back of my neck. "I don't mean to be."

"Eh. Some may say I have an opinion or two of my own." Drew patted the front of my shirt, smoothing invisible wrinkles there. "I've always known that you loved and appreciated me for exactly who I was. Dramatic and loud and opinionated—"

"And vivacious and beautiful and strong."

Drew beamed. "Every partnership has road bumps, but we learned how to navigate them in a way that brought us closer, right? And we learned how to make up." He wiggled his eyebrows. "Remember how you'd buy me those ceramic birds as peace offerings? By the end of our first year together, I had a whole *flock* of geese and chickens and ducks, and I'd started associating poultry with makeup sex."

We both laughed.

The familiar hum of the old refrigerator took over while our laughter faded. I looked around at the farmhouse kitchen, the faded pencil marks from Drew's insistence on measuring the kids' heights over the years, even after they'd become adults. The quirky mushroom-shaped sponge holder that was missing its matching gnome hand soap dispenser after the thing had fallen into the garbage disposal one night when Emma was learning how to clean up after dinner.

The faded spot on the floor where I'd spun Drew around every March fourth in celebration of International Waltz Day. Like many things in the Sunday family, it had started out as a joke. And quickly became family tradition.

"You blew the doors off my world, Drew," I said softly. "You showed me how to be more open-minded. More open-hearted. How beautiful life can be when you're honest about who you are and who you love. You taught me to dream again when I'd forgotten how. And that's why I'm so excited for us to have this next chapter together. Getting to see all of these new places through your eyes… it's going to be phenomenal. And there's no one in the whole world I'd rather experience it with."

Drew kissed me—a kiss filled with love, and memories, and no small amount of the mischief Porter had inherited.

"That's beautiful, honey." Drew's mouth tipped up at one corner, and he pressed a hand to his heart right over Bea Arthur's caftan-face. "Truly beautiful. And I can't tell you how much it means to me to know that I have a partner who values openness and honesty so highly."

"Well, I—"

"Which is why I have to wonder…" Drew peered at me over the tops of his red-framed glasses. "When exactly you planned to tell me that you gave away my cock."

CHAPTER TEN

DREW

Marco squeezed his dark eyes shut, and his shoulders drooped. "You knew."

"Pffft." This was a silly question, so I didn't bother answering it. I'd stared at that rooster fondly every night while making dinner for the better part of two decades and glared at it any time Marco made me mad. I'd recognized it immediately.

It hadn't taken a big-brain genius to figure out how Hawk had come to "buy" it either. No doubt it was the same way I'd been able to "buy" my own freaking caftan at the rummage sale last weekend.

Marco—the man I loved beyond all others—had donated my shit.

I'd considered confronting him about it right there at the rummage sale, but I hadn't.

For one thing, I'd guessed how it had happened, and I knew it wasn't malicious. The last time we'd done a "Keep, Donate, or Toss" session, it had gone about as well as it had today—in other words, I'd steadfastly refused to part with ninety percent of my things. Marco had started out patient, but eventually, he'd thrown up his hands in frustration, carelessly shoved aside the bin we'd been sorting, and bossily declared we were going out for ice cream *right this minute* before his brain melted out of his ears. At some point, he must've grabbed the wrong box when he went back to tidy up, mistaking the unsorted box for a donation box. A simple, careless mistake.

For another, the look of dawning horror and guilt on Marco's face when he'd recognized my caftan at the rummage sale had been pretty compelling. He'd felt genuinely bad that his impatience had led to this, as well he should.

And for yet another, I'd gotten no small amount of amusement out of watching Marco sweat as I'd pretended not to recognize that the caftan was mine and waited for him to admit his mistake.

As I'd told my niece and nephews repeatedly, it didn't do to let your partner get too complacent.

But the real reason I hadn't confronted Marco about it was that I felt bad, too. I had not been handling this whole "downsizing" concept with aplomb.

"And how, ah... how angry would you say you are?" Marco asked with a smile that was both innocently eager and rakishly calculating—a combo I'd found devastating when we'd first met... and only found *more* devastating now. "Because I know where I could get a ceramic rooster for your collection, if you thought that might help."

I huffed out a laugh. God, I loved the man.

"Five out of ten on the anger scale," I told him. "Where ten is how I felt the time you let Hawk juggle with my expensive healing crystals—"

Marco winced.

"—and one is how I felt when you almost referred to my treasures as junk a minute ago," I added pointedly.

He nodded seriously. "Five is good. I can work with five." He hesitated. "And I really am sorry about your things getting donated, baby. It was an accident, and I'm still not entirely sure how it happened, but it wouldn't have happened at all if I hadn't been impatient and careless. I'm trying to work on it, okay? I know this is hard for you. I get it..."

"Do you?" I laughed again, tiredly this time, and lowered myself into the chair Marco had vacated. "Then maybe you can explain it to me. Because here's the thing: I *know* I'm making this difficult. I'm dilly-dallying, which means we've had to press pause on our dream of traveling, and I'm making you feel like the bad guy every time you try to give me a reality check, which is even worse. I hate that."

Marco squatted down beside me, heedless of how the move made his knees pop. "Drew, I don't mean to pressure you—"

"You're not! Or if you are, it's because you know that this is something I want and that I can't wait forever to make it happen. I do want to travel." I took a deep breath and admitted, "But when I start to think about it, I think about all the things we might miss. Hawk planning his wedding to Jack and getting to see them so happy. Porter doing such amazing things with his youth programs. Knox finally letting himself have the future he deserves with Gage. Webb and Luke having more babies. Reed and his sweet Chris coming to visit. Emma, about to graduate and set the world on fire. I don't want to miss those things. So how can I want to stay so badly... and also want to go?"

"Honey, it doesn't have to be black-and-white. You know that. Hell, you *showed* me that. You can have a life that's fun and unexpected, purposeful and *meaningful*, all at the same time. You can have true love while still being dedicated to your family. You don't have to choose." His big hand palmed my knee. "This is no different. When you're ready, *if* you're ready, we'll leave for a while. And then we'll come back as often as you want, for as long as you want, so you can hug your family and love on them. Because those things you're talking about? I don't want to miss them either. Your family is my family, too."

I sniffed. The Universe had been right that summer day all those years ago. Marco was exactly the man I'd needed then. He was the man I needed now.

"But you know what you didn't say just now, Drew?" he went on, his dark eyes serious in his lined face. "In that whole list of things you told me you're going to miss and that you don't want to leave? There wasn't a single mention of your T-shirt collection or your rusty-ass bread pans. It's almost like, deep down, you know that the truly important stuff in this life… isn't stuff." He gave me a half smile. "Christ, I sound like a Hallmark card. This is why I don't do sentimental."

"But you do it so well!" I teased.

He leaned in and held my gaze, though my own was cloudy with tears. "Those trinkets of yours aren't who you are, Drew Sunday. If you need a reminder of the life you've lived, go and ask those kids you raised into wonderful human beings. Ask any person in this wackadoo community you created. Ask the man who's been in love with you since you picked a fight with him over a damn rooster. We'll all be right there to tell you. I, for damn sure, will be *right there* to tell you."

I made a noise that was half chuckle, half sob, and Marco smiled as he ran his thumb under my eye and brushed away the moisture there. Then he kissed me long, and slow, and deep.

"Fuck," I muttered when he finally pulled away. I wiped my eyes with the heels of my hands. "*Fuck.* You've gotten really good at making up. Possibly too good."

"That so? Impossible to stay mad at me, huh?" he teased. "So can we skip to the makeup sex now?"

I laughed. I was more than ready for some makeup sex. More than ready to show this man that, of all the treasures I'd collected over the course of my wonderful life, his heart was the one I valued most.

"Take me home, old man," I said, pushing to my feet and helping Marco to his. "I'll show you that I still know how to wrestle… and win."

As we gathered our things, my eye caught on the rooster, still perched on the sideboard like it had been watching the whole scene unfold with those big golden eyes. That little bird might have brought us together, once upon a time, but now it was only a souvenir.

And not one worth clinging to at the expense of all the memories we still had left to make.

With no hesitation whatsoever, I picked up the rooster, gave him a wink, and set him carefully in the Donate box.

That bird had brought love into my life, a love so strong and true I could only hope it would move on to someone who needed it as much as I had. I had a feeling whoever tripped over it next would add their own story to its history.

I reached over to take Marco's hand, and together, we stepped out into the warm sunshine… toward whatever came next.

Want to meet Reed, the final Sunday brother, and his sweet Chris? Grab The Pretenders of Copper County *HERE → https:// readerlinks.com/l/4135215*

ABOUT MAY ARCHER

May is an M/M author who lives in Boston. She spends her days planning vacations, mainlining diet soda, avoiding the gym, reading M/M romance, and when all other forms of procrastination fail, writing it.

Visit her website at mayarcher.com to sign up for her newsletter to hear about sales and upcoming releases, freebies and behind the scenes info and more! Or join her Facebook group, Club May!

facebook.com/may.archer.author

instagram.com/mayarcherauthor

amazon.com/May-Archer/e/B075JQVGLX

patreon.com/MayArcherRomance

bookbub.com/authors/may-archer

ALSO BY MAY ARCHER

Find me online → https://mayarcher.com/links/

Love in O'Leary Series

Whispering Key Series

The Sunday Brothers Series

Copper County Series

The Way Home Series

Licking Thicket Series

(cowritten with Lucy Lennox)

Champion Security Series

(cowritten with Lucy Lennox)

Honeybridge Series

(cowritten with Lucy Lennox)

For a comprehensive list of titles, audio samples, freebies, suggested reading order, and more, visit my website at www.MayArcher.com!